T. J.'S GHOST

T. J.'S GHOST
by Shirley Climo

Thomas Y. Crowell   New York

T. J.'s Ghost
Text copyright © 1989 by Shirley Climo
Frontispiece copyright © 1989 by Alix R. Berenzy
All rights reserved. No part of this book may be
used or reproduced in any manner whatsoever without
written permission except in the case of brief quotations
embodied in critical articles and reviews. Printed in
the United States of America. For information address
Thomas Y. Crowell Junior Books, 10 East 53rd Street,
New York, N.Y. 10022. Published simultaneously in
Canada by Fitzhenry & Whiteside Limited, Toronto.
Typography by Joyce Hopkins
1 2 3 4 5 6 7 8 9 10
First Edition

Library of Congress Cataloging-in-Publication Data
Climo, Shirley.
  T.J.'s ghost.

  Summary: An eleven-year-old girl helps the ghost
of a nineteenth-century stowaway find a ring that
will help free him to his future.
  [1. Ghosts—Fiction] 1. Title.
PZ7.C62247Taaj 1989   [Fic]   87-42931
ISBN 0-690-04689-8
ISBN 0-690-04691-X (lib. bdg.)

For Theresa, Junior—the real T.J.—
who once said, "Tell me a ghost story!"

T. J.'S GHOST

1

"Ouch!"

T.J. dropped the cat. She didn't mean to, but all of a sudden five cat toenails were digging through the sleeve of her pajamas. Flotsam landed with a thud and then dashed across the kitchen floor to rub her whiskers against Auntie Onion's bare ankles.

"Snakes alive!"

Auntie Onion jumped, almost knocking over the coffeepot with her elbow, and stamped her left foot on Flotsam's tail. The cat yowled.

"Drat that Flotsam!" cried Auntie Onion. "I thought sure I felt a mouse!"

"Here, Sam! Nice Sam," coaxed T.J., crooning the cat's nickname as she tried to catch hold of her.

But Flotsam flattened her ears and stalked beneath the kitchen table.

Auntie Onion pulled a bandanna from her bathrobe pocket and dabbed her forehead. "Such a fright to start the day!"

"Something spooked Sam, too," T.J. mumbled through a yawn. "And not a mouse."

She squinted at her great-aunt. Talk about frights! The hem of Auntie Onion's bathrobe dangled unevenly below her knees, showing skinny birdlike legs that ended in tennis shoes with the laces missing. Gray hair frizzled about her face like little electric wires. Her old-fashioned hearing aid was missing, too. No pink cord trailed from her ear.

"Seeing you is another surprise," Auntie Onion continued. "Whatever made you get up so early?"

"You did!" T.J. said loudly. She tiptoed across the chilly vinyl floor and lifted a corner of the tablecloth. Sam stared up at her with wide yellow eyes.

"Did?" Auntie Onion looked confused. "Did what?"

"Made me get up. 'T.J., T.J.' I heard you call me."

Auntie Onion turned down the blue flame beneath the percolator and poured a cup of coffee. The steam clouded her glasses, and she aimed misted lenses in T.J.'s direction. "I never did any such thing!" she declared, as indignant as the cat.

"Well, *someone* called me. *'Tee-Jay-a-ay!'* Just like

that." T.J. glared back at her aunt. "Weird!"

"Most older houses groan a bit, like most older folk." Auntie Onion bobbed her head. "Noises are nothing to get het up about."

"Who's het up?" asked T.J. "But whatever it was made Sam so jumpy she scratched me." T.J. pushed up her sleeve. "See? Claw marks."

Auntie Onion blew on her coffee and peered over the rim of the cup at the red spots on T.J.'s arm. "Flea bites! Bound to happen with Flotsam as a bedfellow. And one of these mornings you may wake up with more than a few fleas for company!"

T.J. grinned and patted Sam. The cat's orange and white and black fur bulged around the middle. "Kittens!"

"Bitten, like I said," agreed Auntie Onion.

T.J. didn't bother answering. Conversations with her great-aunt were crazy, especially before she'd plugged in her hearing aid. T.J. pulled a bowl from the dishwasher, filled it with Rice Krispies, and splashed on some milk. The cereal floated like chips of driftwood in a milky sea.

"Not even one little pop," muttered T.J. as she sat down at the table. Remembering to raise her voice, she added, "The Krispies are stale. DAMP!"

"Lamp!" cried Auntie Onion. "Now, aren't you clever! My earpiece!"

T.J. looked up. Auntie Onion's hearing aid swung from the imitation ship's lantern overhead.

"Always try to put the dratted thing where I'll see it first thing in the morning." Auntie Onion jerked down the hearing aid, attached the cord to the battery in her bathrobe pocket, and adjusted the button in her ear. "That's better!" She tried a sip of coffee. "A mite weak, but hot enough to take the chill off my bones."

T.J. shivered. She needed something to take the chill off *her* bones. The day was gray, and beads of water trickled down the windowpane.

"I thought you said it didn't rain in California in the summer."

"That's just mist," Auntie Onion replied. "It will lift by noon. Unless . . ." She took another swallow of coffee. ". . . unless we get caught in a spell of fog."

T.J. pushed a slice of bread into the toaster. "A spell of fog," she repeated. The words had a mysterious flavor. Then, almost in answer to her thoughts, she heard it again. Faint and far away, something like a siren sounded.

"Listen! Maybe that's what woke me up!"

"What?" Auntie Onion cocked her head.

"That—horn! You know, those warning signals they send out from lighthouses."

"Don't hear a thing." Auntie Onion took off her glasses and polished them on her bathrobe. "Anyway, the Coast Guard turned off the foghorn at Pigeon Point years ago."

"But I *heard* it!"

Auntie Onion chuckled. "Likely heard your Uncle Will. He snores like an old bull elephant seal."

Smoke curled up from the toaster. T.J. fished out her toast and painted over the burned spots with strawberry jam. "A genuine foghorn," she insisted.

"You've been watching too much T.V. Can't tell what's real and what isn't," said Auntie Onion. She opened the kitchen window and helped Sam out over the sill and into the lemon bush. There weren't any lemons on it, but the branches made a good cat ladder.

Auntie Onion sat down opposite T.J. "Now, when I was a girl, there was no such thing as television. Didn't even have a radio for quite a while. We made our own fun—"

The telephone rang and Auntie Onion stopped mid sentence. T.J. noticed that she could hear *that* ring well enough.

"Hello!" Auntie Onion shouted into the phone, catching the wire from her hearing aid in the curly telephone cord. "Is that you, Norma?"

Once she got started, her aunt could talk forever on the phone. "Okay if I go down to the beach?" asked T.J.

"A fine kettle of goldfish!" Auntie Onion struggled to untangle the cords. "Hold on, Norma!" She straightened her hearing aid and turned to T.J. Her eyebrows puckered together over the nosepiece of her glasses. "Well, suit yourself. But wear a sweater."

7

Suit yourself. In the two days she'd been here, her aunt must have said that twenty times. T.J. nodded and shoved back from the table. She took giant steps across the floor to the back stairs, as if she were already jumping waves.

"And don't go near the water!" Auntie Onion shook the receiver in her hand. "No, of course I wasn't talking to you, Norma," she apologized. "Speak up, will you? This connection is dreadful."

The gloomy upstairs hall gave T.J. the creeps. There wasn't any carpet covering the dark floorboards, and the splotchy brown wallpaper reminded her of dried oatmeal. She tiptoed past Uncle Will's closed door and through her own open one. Hers was always open. The door had warped, and it swung ajar on its hinges even after she'd given it a good slam. But everything in this house seemed to tilt. It was a bungalow. That meant the upstairs was only half a story high and the roof sloped down to meet the walls. The slanted ceiling above her bed was so low that she'd cracked her head when she jumped up this morning.

The fog outside her dim window was thick as marshmallow creme. T.J. could scarcely make out the red heads of the geraniums that poked above the picket fence, and the branches of the eucalyptus tree were no more than dark pencil lines against the gray. The sand dunes had disappeared completely in the mist.

"Tee-Jay!"

Maybe it was just the wind. T.J. pressed her cheek against the cold windowpane, not even daring to breathe. Nothing. The air was heavy, still, muffling even the sound of the surf against the rocks.

T.J. blew out her breath in disgust. "Jelly brain!" she said aloud.

She dug a sweatshirt from the dresser drawer. It felt damp already, and the jeans she pulled on clung, limp and clammy, to her legs. T.J. picked up a hairbrush, but only swacked a couple of times at the snarls in her hair. It didn't matter how she looked. She didn't know anyone around here.

So how did the foghorn know her name?

That was crazy. Or else she was. But no one could blame her for that. If it wasn't for her mom's job, she would be having a perfectly normal summer in Cleveland right now.

Usually, Mom's job was no big deal. If her mother wanted to sell real estate, that was all right with T.J., so long as she didn't sell *their* house. Then this June Mom had sold a big, redbrick mansion in Shaker Heights. You'd think she'd rented out the White House, because just for unloading an old eyesore, her mother had won a trip to Hawaii for two. Lucky Mom. Lucky Dad. Not-so-lucky T.J. She'd practically been dumped on Auntie Onion's doorstep.

"There's a famous lighthouse nearby," her mother

9

had said. "You'll love staying with dear old Auntie Onion!" Mom had run the name all together, like someone in a nursery rhyme. Dear-Old-Auntie-Onion!

Auntie Onion was certainly old. She was Mom's father's sister, and that made her ancient enough to be an ancestor. Even Uncle Will looked like he'd rowed over on the *Mayflower*. T.J. was the only thing in the whole house that didn't creak. Two weeks here were going to seem like forever.

T.J. was tying her shoes when she heard it again.

"Tee-Jay-a-ay!"

No mistaking that. The first tone was high and short, the second low and long. "Tee-Jay-a-ay!" the foghorn pleaded.

A prickle began at the end of T.J.'s backbone and worked its way up to her neck. She jerked a shoelace so hard that it broke and she had to double knot the frayed end.

"Okay, okay," she whispered in answer. "I'm coming."

She had to find out if that foghorn really was blowing. If it wasn't, and she had flipped, no telling what she'd hear next. Fire sirens. Clocks striking thirteen. Anyway, she'd rather freeze down by the ocean than mold like a mushroom in this gloomy room.

Before she started down the stairs, T.J. remembered to grab her sweater. In the kitchen, Auntie Onion was still shouting into the phone.

"A shame!" her great-aunt exclaimed. "But nothing to twist your knickers over."

Twist your knickers? Whatever that meant, she could bet Auntie Onion was talking about her.

T.J. opened the kitchen door and stepped out into the fog.

2

When she reached the picket fence that edged the backyard, T.J. stopped and looked back at the house. The low-hanging mist blurred everything, as if she were squinting through a plastic shower curtain. There was a glow from the kitchen window of the bungalow. Another light, shimmering like a halo above the darkness of the roof, shone from the porthole of the Crow's Nest. T.J. could make out Uncle Will, his face pressed against the glass pane like a jack-o'-lantern.

She had never seen a real crow's nest. T.J. supposed she might see the bird's nest sometime, but sailing ships no longer had lookouts perched on top of masts. Uncle Will said modern boats used radar instead. He called his tower room a crow's nest because it was up so high and had such a good view, with round windows all around. From down here it didn't look very shiplike. It was more like a humongous toadstool growing out of the roof.

Uncle Will was shouting something at her. Maybe he wanted to come along, but T.J. would rather he didn't. Uncle Will had already told her more about the Pacific Ocean than she cared to know.

T.J. cupped her hands and yelled, "I can't hear you!" Then she turned around and opened the gate.

The trail to the beach twisted around bushes and was overgrown with brown spiky thistles. Twigs caught at T.J.'s jeans, sprinkling them with moisture, and her canvas shoes were drenched.

"Some mist!" said T.J., scowling up at the sky. "In Ohio we call this a drizzle."

A prickly leaf snagged her sweater, and she stopped to jerk it free. That's when she saw Flotsam. The cat sat right in the middle of the path.

"Sam! Were you waiting for me?"

In answer, Flotsam got up and picked her way down the path, her tail curled like a question mark over her back. She moved swiftly, not bothering to sniff at gopher holes, as if she had no time to waste on foolishness.

A few yards farther on, the brambles disappeared and only beach grass struggled to survive in the salty ground. Then the sand dunes began, rolling like giant waves down to the ocean itself. Flotsam walked lightly over the sand, but T.J.'s shoes sank in with every step, and she had to scramble to keep up with the cat.

The last dune sloped down to the narrow beach. The sand was strewn with pebbles and edged with driftwood tossed up by winter storms. The tide had started to come in, but the gray waves made no more noise than the gray clouds above. Although the bright beam from the lighthouse at Pigeon Point cut through the gloom at intervals, the beach was still as a graveyard. She and Sam were all alone.

Even with her sweater buttoned up to her chin, T.J. shivered. She wished Jana were here. She could really use a friend right now. Jana would call this an adventure.

"*The Super Sleuths and the Case of the Vanishing Foghorn*," T.J. exclaimed.

What a great title for their book! Chapter One of the mystery she and Jana were writing was almost finished. They hadn't figured out what would happen next, but Jana said that was part of the mystery. Neither one of them could think of a title. It was Jana's idea to call themselves the Super Sleuths. T.J. had thought of having a secret code to thicken the plot. They had hardly even begun to work on words before she'd had to leave. Jana acted like it didn't even matter.

"Mega!" Jana had squealed when T.J. told her she was going to California. "Maybe you'll meet a hunk on the beach!"

"A hunk of what?" T.J.'d asked her.

"A guy!" Jana had smiled. "Everything begins in California. Valley talk and all those awesome new words. Shaky. Dyno. Jelly brain."

Even then, T.J. had had a hunch that her California vacation might not turn out as Jana predicted. Now she was sure of it.

"Make a list of any new words you hear," Jana had insisted. "We'll use them in our secret code."

Jana had just been trying to cheer her up. T.J. could bet she had already forgotten about their book. Lately all she cared about was T.J.'s brother. Dave had just turned sixteen, and Jana thought he was the greatest. Whenever she came over, Jana eyeballed Dave and his junker car. There wasn't any mystery about that.

T.J. kicked up a shower of damp sand. How could she learn any new words when there wasn't anyone to talk to? But she didn't need Jana. She could take care of herself. And of Sam, too.

Flotsam darted off across the sand to inspect a strand of seaweed. T.J. followed, stamping on the strings of kelp. The fat brown pods burst beneath her heels with loud, satisfying pops. Flotsam pricked up her ears, but continued to prowl along the shore. She ignored the sassy gulls that swooped low over her head, and she stopped only to shake drops of water from her paws.

Maybe Sam had a good reason, a *cat's* reason, for hanging around, but T.J. didn't. There wasn't any foghorn. Even beachcombing wasn't much fun. The ocean was too cold for any cones or cowries or those twisted shells you held up to your ear to hear the sea. But she wouldn't mind finding an abalone shell. Uncle Will had a big one in his curio cabinet. Shades of pink and green gleamed like a rainbow in the silvery lining of the shell. An abalone would look neat in her aquarium at home.

T.J. left Sam and wandered down the beach. She picked up a few chalky clamshells and some purple mussels, good sized but chipped. She stuffed them in her sweater pocket. She found quite a few slivers of green glass and a pretty yellow piece, polished by the waves until its edges were round and smooth. Colored glass would be nice in her aquarium, too, mixed in with all the pebbles at the bottom.

Then she spotted a chunk of blue glass. Sea blue, or the color the sea was supposed to be. T.J. glanced uneasily at the ocean. Already the dark waves had begun to take bigger bites from the shore.

"Don't go near the water!"

That's what Auntie Onion had warned. T.J. couldn't help it if the water was coming nearer to her, but she had better go back. She picked up the piece of blue glass, jammed it into her pocket, and turned around. There wasn't a sign of Sam.

"Here, kitty!" T.J. called.

A gull shrieked in answer.

At the base of the dune, above the waterline, was a log, bleached white by sun and salt. Perhaps

Sam was napping behind it. But no cat slept in its shelter, and T.J. only startled a lizard.

She took off her sweater and hung it carefully on the log's gnarled arm. She wasn't going to chance losing her shells and glass while she searched for Flotsam. Not that Flotsam wasn't important. A vanishing cat was more of a mystery than some signal from a foghorn that wasn't even there. T.J. started across the sand, yelling "Sam!" as she went.

And then the foghorn blew, so loud, so close, that T.J. stuck her fingers in her ears and screamed.

Ears plugged, eyes shut, T.J. waited for the howling to stop.

For Pete's sake! She must be fog struck! That horrible noise was coming from her own mouth.

T.J. snapped her jaws together, almost biting her tongue. At least she hadn't begun seeing things, too. The beach was truly deserted now, for her screams had scattered the gulls. Maybe Flotsam had gotten tired of being dive-bombed by those birds and had gone home. That cat was a lot smarter than she was.

T.J. headed back to the old log and was about to pick up her sweater when she distinctly heard a meow. Only Sam mewed in such a funny way, like she'd swallowed a frog. T.J. whirled around.

To her left, beyond the small cove where the waves broke against the boulders, T.J. saw a boy. He was perched on the largest of the flat-topped rocks, looking out to sea. T.J. was positive he had not been there a couple of minutes ago.

The boy was dressed in some sort of skimpy tank top, and his dungarees were torn off at the knees. Shreds, Jana would call them. He was drenched, besides. Even his hair was dripping. It hung straight to his shoulders, dark red in color, as if it had rusted from swimming in salt water. But that wasn't the only reason that T.J. gawked. In his arms, the boy clutched a calico cat.

"Sam!" T.J. cried.

3

The boy spun about and stared at T.J.

T.J. stared back, practicing in her head what she'd say. She'd accuse that boy of stealing Sam. She would come right out and call him a . . . a catnapper! She put her hands on her hips, stuck out her chin, and took a deep breath. But when she opened her mouth, the voice that came out was little and squeaky. "Can I please have my cat?"

The boy did not answer. He narrowed his eyes with suspicion and tightened his grip on Flotsam.

A fine kettle of goldfish! thought T.J. Even Sam was looking at her through slitted, sleepy lids, as if T.J. were the stranger. But she couldn't just stand here as if she'd been planted. T.J. took a few cautious steps forward. "Here, Sam," she called. "Good kitty."

The boy shook his head. "How come you know her name?" he asked in a husky voice.

"Because Sam's my cat. Or practically mine."

"Sam's my cat. Or practically mine," he echoed, and then added, "Though I had not hoped to set hands on her again." He'd cleared his throat, but he still spoke in a peculiar way. He dropped his *h*'s and pronounced his *a*'s like *i*'s. Sam sounded like *Sim* and *cat* came out like *kite*, as if he had a wad of bubblegum in his cheek. "I feared this cat joined Davy Jones long ago."

Davy Jones? How did he get into this? T.J. looked over her shoulder. Maybe this guy had a friend hiding somewhere. Maybe a whole gang. Perhaps he'd grabbed Flotsam just to trick her, and then he'd grab her next. . . .

"Surely you've heard tell of Davy Jones?" the boy asked. He stood up, not loosening his hold on the cat, and balanced on his toes on the rock. "He's the old man at the bottom of the sea."

"I don't know what in the world you're talking about," T.J. retorted. "Just give me my cat."

"Ain't yours. Samantha here's the ship's cat."

"Her name is Flotsam!" T.J. was beginning to get mad. "And she's my great-aunt's personal property, that's what she is."

T.J. picked her way across the fringe of beach

20

that separated her from Sam and the boy. The soles of her shoes made wavy lines in the damp sand, and already the half-moons left by the heels were filling with water. How come that boy hadn't left any footprints? He couldn't have dropped out of the sky like a gull!

The boy stood there, grinning, watching her approach. She had to watch where she stepped and avoid the larger stones, slippery with moss. It was hard to be dignified when she had to scramble sideways, like a crab. But he didn't look so hot, either. He looked positively blue with cold. A soaking-wet scarecrow stuck on a rock.

When T.J. was almost close enough to reach out and snatch Flotsam, the boy deliberately moved back on the boulder. "Begging your pardon, Miss," he said politely, "but I traveled all the way from Sydney Town with this particular cat and I'll not give her up now."

T.J. glared at him. "You've made a mistake," she began. Then she forgot all about being mad—or scared—because she'd suddenly thought of a terrific title for her and Jana's book. *"A Case of Mistaken Identity!"* she finished firmly. "Cat look-alikes. Could be your cat is a relative of mine."

"Not bloomin' likely at all!" he retorted rudely. "Since Sydney is in New South Wales, in Australia."

An Aussie! No wonder he sounded strange. They'd

21

studied Australia in school last year. Kangaroos and wombats.

"So?" said T.J. "I'm from Cleveland. That's in Ohio, in the U.S.A. Sam's American, too. Uncle Will found her right here on the beach. She was just a tiny kitten. He named her Flotsam because that's stuff you find floating in the water."

The boy sat down again and cradled the cat protectively. "She seems to know me well enough," he said as Sam nestled against his wet shoulder.

Flotsam was being no help at all! At the very least you'd think she'd scratch him. "You better not squeeze her," T.J. warned. "She's going to have kittens."

"Kittens!" The boy looked at the cat in alarm and relaxed his grip. "It may be so," he said after a moment. "It may be as you say . . . mistaken identity." He put Flotsam down gently. At once she began to investigate the rocks for any little hidden crabs that might be hiding in the crevices. He watched her, rubbing his nose with a knuckle. "I wished so hard you were Samantha that I misled myself," he said.

Without warm Sam to hug, he looked colder than ever. T.J. took another step forward. "I guess you call your cat Sam," she asked, "because it's short for Samantha?"

The boy nodded, but kept his eyes on the cat. "Kittens!" he repeated.

"Two cats called Sam! That's funny if you think

about it." He did not answer, and she tried again. "I'm called T.J."

"T.J.? Queer name for a jill." He gazed at her. "And queerer yet to see a jill in trousers."

"These aren't trousers. They're jeans. Pants. And Jill isn't my name. It's really Theresa."

He laughed. "And jill means girl." The boy climbed down from the rock. "Pleased to make your acquaintance, Miss Theresa."

"Same here," said T.J., shaking his hand. The coldness of his fingers sent a shiver down her spine. "You ought to go back where you're staying and get warmed up."

"Aye," he agreed, "but that I cannot do until I find what I'm looking for."

"A calico cat!" declared T.J. "And I'll help you look."

He shook his head. "I'm searching for something different."

"I was beachcombing earlier. For shells." She pointed toward her sweater. "I'm pretty good at finding things."

"I must settle this business myself." He hesitated. " 'Tis a gold ring I'm missing."

"A lost ring, in all this sand?" T.J. threw up her hands. "That'll be worse than trying to find the prize in Cracker Jacks."

"Crack-a-jack?" he asked. "Now that means good. . . ." He stopped, looking puzzled. "Is it possible you mean a Jack-tar, like myself?"

How did tar get into it? T.J. shrugged her shoulders. Talking with this guy was worse than talking with Auntie Onion.

"Jack-tar is ship talk for sailor," he explained.

"Oh!" T.J. nodded. If he was a sailor, that made sense, except that he didn't look old enough. He could have lied about his age when he joined up. Or else he could be lying about everything right now.

He flushed as if she'd spoken aloud. "It was not official, my signing on." The color drained from his face, leaving it even paler than before. "Although I'm signed off, right enough."

"I don't see how you got off if you weren't on," T.J. objected. She scanned the ocean. "And I don't see any ship."

"Then fault the fog." He ran his fingers through his red hair. "But I had a vessel, and that's the truth, sure as you see me standing here. She was bound from Sydney to San Francisco and called the *Coya*."

"The what?"

She wished he'd talk more slowly. With his funny words, and that funny accent, she had trouble keeping up. But before he could repeat it, the foghorn bellowed. Both of them started.

"There! You heard it too!" cried T.J.

"Aye. 'Tis the horn from the lighthouse at Pigeon Point."

24

"Does it talk to you? I mean, can you tell what it's saying?" T.J. asked.

"To me it cries, 'Come back! Come back!' "

"I thought it said my name," T.J. admitted. " 'Tee-Jay-a-ay!' "

"Only special ones can hear its voice at all." The boy smiled at her as if they shared a secret. "And then only in a spell of fog."

"Why me?" T.J. puzzled. "I'm no one special. I'm average in everything except history, and I'm terrible in that."

Flotsam interrupted her with a howl. The incoming tide had stranded the cat on a rock. Waves licked at her legs, and she twitched her paws, raising her voice in protest.

"Get your cat!" the boy ordered. "Hurry!"

T.J. waited until an especially large wave had washed in and out. Then she worked her way over to Sam and picked up the cat. The fog was lifting slightly, and a thin shaft of sunlight cut through the overcast. The boy looked up, suddenly anxious. "You'd better go home." His eyes rested for a moment on Flotsam. "*Both* of you."

"Yeah," T.J. agreed. Let him be bossy. No cat in its right mind would stay here now, and neither should she. Her shoes were already so full of water that they needed bailing out. Each new wave splashed higher on the rocks, and, as it ebbed, pulled and tugged at her legs.

25

She clasped Flotsam in both arms and walked cautiously, head down, checking each foothold before she stepped. Once she slipped, plunging her left foot down between two rocks. The stones gripped her ankle like pliers, but, with the next wave, T.J. jerked her foot free. She was glad she'd double-knotted the shoelace, but the skin was scraped raw above the canvas top.

The beach below the log was almost entirely under water. Only a narrow neck of sand edged the dunes, and that was already scalloped with a foamy scum. T.J. climbed the first rise and flopped down, panting. She had not even said good-bye to that sailor, if that's what he was.

"What was the name of your ship again?" she called. Maybe Uncle Will would know it.

There was no answer. She pushed up on one elbow and looked back. Waves surged over the top of the boulder where he had been. The boy himself had disappeared.

T.J. stood up and draped the cat about her neck like a fur piece. Flotsam relaxed, letting her legs dangle, and began purring loudly in T.J.'s right ear. When it came to cats, she was a special one.

"I'm glad I didn't lose you," murmured T.J., starting up the dune.

4

As soon as she'd reached the patch of brambles, T.J. spotted Uncle Will. He was jogging down the path, frowning at the pocket watch in his hand. As he hurried, the tufts of silver hair on his head blew straight up. He looked like the white rabbit in *Alice in Wonderland*.

"Hi!" called T.J.

"So there you are!" answered Uncle Will. "I was just about to call the Coast Guard."

He seemed cross. She had never seen him be anything but jolly before. His face was almost always crinkled in a smile. Now the corners of his mouth drooped down.

"I'm sorry," said T.J., although she wasn't sure what she should be apologizing for.

"I told you to come back before high tide."

T.J. was genuinely surprised. "I didn't hear you."

"I'm sure you saw me at the window. But you didn't try very hard to listen." He looked at T.J.'s soggy shoes.

"I slipped," she murmured, unwrapping Flotsam from around her neck. The cat immediately ducked beneath a bush and began to lick the salt from her fur.

"Well, now you listen to this. Don't fool with the tide, or it will fool you. That's the first lesson you've got to learn."

T.J. ducked her head. She hadn't disobeyed on purpose, but it was impossible to explain anything to anyone today. She followed Uncle Will in silence back to the house. On the doorstep, he stopped and waggled his finger.

"Less said to your aunt the better. She's already as fussed as a mackerel in a minnow net."

As they came in the kitchen door, Auntie Onion looked up from the chopping board and waved the large knife in her hand. "There you are!" she exclaimed when she saw T.J., just as Uncle Will had done. "I told myself you'd be home for lunch, seeing as how your breakfast was so skimpy." She glanced at T.J.'s feet. "Change into your slippers."

"Okay," agreed T.J., glad for the chance to escape up to her room. When she came down again, the kitchen was steamy and smelled of frying onions.

"Clam chowder," said Auntie Onion as she stirred a bubbling pot.

"Good," said T.J. with more enthusiasm than she felt.

All of her great-aunt's concoctions tasted the same. Oniony. No matter what the recipe called for, she managed to sneak in some onions to "perk things up." T.J. didn't mind onion on a hamburger, or even snips of green ones decorating a salad. But Auntie Onion added them to absolutely everything, except orange juice. Her aunt's real name was Elizabeth, but her nickname fit her like an onion skin.

Uncle Will was waiting, with his napkin tucked under his chin and his elbows on the table. When Auntie Onion placed a bowl of chowder before him, he sniffed it suspiciously. Then he turned to T.J. and whispered loudly, "This is one of your aunt's favorite games. It's called Find-the-Clam-in-the-Chowder."

T.J. grinned. He was wearing his good mood again.

"She uses a secret formula, but I'll share it," he went on. "Take one potato, scrub it. Add one clam, chop it. Then stew 'em up with a half dozen onions."

"Peel them," suggested T.J.

"You got it!" said Uncle Will, but Auntie Onion just snapped, "Poppycock!" and slammed a bowl of oyster crackers between them on the table.

T.J. took a spoonful of the chowder. It was creamy on her tongue and tasted a lot better than it smelled. A lump of butter melted in the middle of the soup. Outside the kitchen window, the sun, like another golden puddle, shone faintly through the fog. So far, neither Uncle Will nor Auntie Onion had questioned her about the morning. That was just fine with T.J., but it was too good to last.

Uncle Will put down his spoon and cleared his throat. "I've posted a timetable for the tides by the telephone."

T.J. swiveled in her chair and stretched her neck to see. The tidal chart looked like a bus schedule, or like one of those screens in an airport that lists the hours for takeoffs and landings. It was set up like a calendar, with the month and days of the week marked. High and low tides were listed for both day and night, down to the exact minute. Apparently an ocean was more reliable than an airplane and was never late coming in or going out. Today was August 14, and high tide had been at ten fifty-three. T.J. had found that out for herself.

She dropped a handful of oyster crackers into her chowder. "Thanks," she said. "I'll be sure to check it out before I go down to the shore."

"Not today," said Auntie Onion. "For twenty-four hours you're beached."

"Your aunt means grounded," corrected Uncle Will. "You'll have to stay in."

"Grounded!" T.J. protested through a mouthful

of crackers. "Just because I got a little wet?"

"Consider yourself lucky." Auntie Onion waggled a finger. "You might have gotten more than a dunking."

"The most important thing to remember," said Uncle Will solemnly, "is never turn your back on the ocean."

T.J. stirred her soup. "I'll be careful this time," she promised. "And the tide's starting to go out anyway." She pointed to the timetable. "I sort of told this guy I met on the beach that I'd help him look for something."

"You shouldn't talk to strangers!" exclaimed Auntie Onion.

"He was nice. Not at first, but later on. I couldn't always understand him because of his accent."

Auntie Onion and Uncle Will exchanged glances. "Perhaps he's staying at the hostel at Pigeon Point," Uncle Will suggested. "They get young people from all over."

"How old is he?" asked Auntie Onion.

"Bigger than me." Auntie Onion looked alarmed by her answer, so she added, "But not much. Thirteen or fourteen." If she wanted to get back to the beach, ever again, she'd better change the subject. T.J. tipped her soup bowl to get the last swallow and said, "I left in a hurry and forgot my sweater. It's got shells and stuff in the pocket."

"More's the pity," said Auntie Onion, "since you're beached until tomorrow afternoon."

31

"My blue sweater's almost new. Mom will be mad if I lose it."

"Then I'll get it," said Uncle Will, pushing back from the table.

T.J. sighed. So much for Auntie Onion's "suit yourself." Something had to suit her before it was suitable for you. She was stuck here. "What can I do?"

"First of all you can do the dishes," her aunt said brightly. "You wash and I'll dry."

Auntie Onion wrapped T.J. in an enormous apron that had "KISS THE COOK" written across the bib. Then she upended a bottle of liquid soap into the sink and turned on the tap. The suds billowed over the basin.

Talk about high tide! T.J. could drown standing right here in the kitchen. "Is the dishwasher broken?" she asked.

"Not that I know of," Auntie Onion replied. "But it's not very reliable either, since I forget to turn it on." She shook her head. "Other times I'll run the dratted thing through twice. This way we'll know for sure that the job's done and everything's hunky-dory."

Hunky-dory! That's not what T.J. would call it. She'd have dishpan hands for the rest of the summer. She groaned loudly, but Auntie Onion didn't hear, or pretended not to. She began unloading glasses and bowls from the dishwasher and piling them on the sinkboard for T.J. to wash. Most were the thick pottery pieces that you bought at discount drugstores, but a few were so fragile you could almost see right through the pattern of rosebuds. T.J. handled those carefully, but Auntie Onion dried everything the same—just a shake and then a swipe with the dish towel. T.J. was washing the last pot, trying to scrape the burned onions from the bottom, when Uncle Will burst through the door.

" 'Home is the sailor, home from sea,' " he announced cheerfully. "Didn't see a living soul on the beach, either. But I did find your sweater on that old log, still high and dry." He dropped it on the chair.

T.J. left the pot to soak clean and wiped her hands on the apron. "I hope I didn't lose that blue glass."

One by one she began pulling her treasures from the pocket and lining them up on the kitchen table. The clamshells. The pieces of green glass and the smooth yellow one. The blue glass! Some mussels, most of them chipped. At the bottom of her pocket, caught in the seam, T.J. felt another shell. She dug it out and set it down beside the others.

"What's that?" asked Uncle Will.

T.J. shrugged. She didn't even recall finding it.

Uncle Will picked it up and turned it over in the palm of his hand. "It looks like an Amoria Zebra!" His face got quite pink. "A zebra volute," he explained to T.J., as if that helped.

"It is pretty," she agreed. The shell wasn't very

big, only an inch or so long, but it was creamy gold in color with dark stripes. "And it does sort of look like a zebra."

"That's not the point!" Uncle Will was practically shouting now. "If I'm not mistaken, this shell has come all the way from Australia!"

5

T.J. put the striped shell on her dresser. The pale sunlight that filtered through her window made the shell glow as if a tiny night-light shone inside it. T.J. studied it thoughtfully. She certainly should remember finding it. She wondered if she *had* gone batty.

Or wombatty.

T.J. grinned. That was a great word, even if she had made it up herself. She could tell Jana everybody said it out west.

She might as well start that word list while she was grounded. Heck, she had enough time on her hands to practically write an encyclopedia. T.J. reached for the pad of yellow paper and a pencil. The paper was already lined, so it would be easy to set up the word list like a tide table. All she had to do was leave spaces between the date and the phrase and the meaning.

Aug. 14 A.M.	Snakes alive!	Wow!
Aug. 14 A.M.	A fine kettle of goldfish!	A mess!
Aug. 14 A.M.	Twist your knickers	Get upset

She had to look up knickers in the dictionary. Knickers were old-fashioned underwear. Knee-length bloomers! Maybe Auntie Onion still wore them. Bloomers reminded her of *bloomin'* and that sent her mind back to that Australian boy all over again.

Maybe he had returned to the beach. The tide must be low by now. What if Flotsam had gone back, too? She'd never come in for the spoonful of clam chowder that T.J. had put in her kitty bowl.

T.J. went over to the window. The wooden sash was warped and the window squealed as she pushed it up. Then it stuck, but at least it was open wide enough for her to put her head out. That was all of her that was going to get out again today.

Only a few wisps of fog remained, and the backyard looked inviting. T.J. sniffed. That Vicks salve smell came from the eucalyptus tree. Auntie Onion said that fleas didn't like the odor. Tomorrow she'd pick some of those leaves and put them under her mattress pad.

The geraniums looked like a line of red-capped soldiers marching along the fence. Beyond, T.J. could see the brambles, then the dunes, and in the distance a band of blue where the ocean washed against the sky. T.J. squinted. The leaves on the brambles were shaking. Something was definitely crawling beneath them.

"Auntie Onion!" she shouted as a gray head poked up from among the branches.

Her aunt looked up, waved in all directions, and then bent beneath the bushes again.

"Hey!" T.J. cupped her hands. "Are you looking for Sam?"

"Flotsam?" Auntie Onion straightened up. "That cat can look out for herself."

"But the last time I saw her she went into those bushes. Maybe she's lost again!"

"Again?" Auntie Onion shook the wire on her hearing aid as if she didn't believe her ears. "Flotsam's never strayed far in all her nine lives."

T.J. swallowed. She hadn't told Auntie Onion or Uncle Will that the boy had almost stolen Sam, and she certainly wasn't about to bring it up now. "Then what are you looking for?" she yelled.

"Raspberries." Auntie Onion pulled a wicker basket from underneath a bush.

So that's what those prickly brambles were! "Where are the berries?" T.J. asked.

"The biggest and best grow underneath the leaves," said Auntie Onion. "Smart berries. That way the birds won't snatch them." She stooped and then held up a berry between two fingers.

The raspberry was so large, so fat, that T.J. couldn't miss seeing it, even from her perch in her bedroom window. Her mouth watered. Mom hardly ever bought raspberries in the store because they were too expensive. "I can come out and help you," T.J. offered.

"You can, but you can't," Auntie Onion answered. "Because you're grounded."

"But I'd be right there on the ground," T.J. pointed out.

Auntie Onion cocked her head and considered for a minute. Then, "It's logical," she agreed, "but I don't believe it's allowable. Why don't you go pester your Uncle Will instead?"

Pester! That was the thanks she got for volunteering to help! T.J. slammed the window and went back to her word list.

August 14 A.M.   Jack-tar   A sailor

T.J. glanced up at the shell. Maybe she *would* go up to the Crow's Nest. She had something important to ask Uncle Will, and that certainly wasn't being a pest.

Getting up to the Crow's Nest was a genuine adventure. At the top of the back stairs was a skinny door with an "Off Limits!" sign swinging from the doorknob. When you opened it, there was a circular iron staircase to climb. The steps were slippery rungs, like a ship's ladder, with a railing, twisted like a rope, winding alongside. All of a sudden your head would poke through a hole in the ceiling, and there you'd be, in this secret tower room. It wasn't much larger than a clothes closet back home, but it was big enough for a table, messy with charts and papers, a curved-back captain's chair, some bookshelves, and a curio cabinet in one corner. T.J. couldn't figure out how her uncle had squeezed so much into so little, or how he'd gotten all of it up there to begin with.

"Awesome!" T.J. had declared when she saw it on the day she arrived.

"Awful!" Auntie Onion had corrected from the foot of the staircase. She didn't like high places and claimed that only the direst emergency would make her venture up there.

Uncle Will seemed to be expecting T.J., or else he'd heard her coming. "Welcome aboard!" He snapped to attention, touching one finger to the brim of his sea captain's hat. Then he stooped and fiddled with the knob on his spyglass. The glass was mounted in front of one of the portholes, on a swivel, so that he could turn it from side to side. "I've got the focus right on Pigeon Point. You can see the lighthouse plain as your finger before your nose."

T.J. peered through the lens. The lighthouse, perched on a rocky outcrop, did indeed look like a tall white finger, poking up to hold the sky away from the sea. "I don't see any pigeons flying around," she said.

"That's not how Pigeon Point got its name. That headland's called after the *Carrier Pigeon*. A fine clipper ship she was, out of Boston on her maiden voyage. She went down right off this coast."

"How come?" asked T.J.

"Fog. The same reason for most of the ship-wrecks, and the reason why the lighthouse stands there today."

"And a foghorn," said T.J.

Uncle Will gave her a peculiar look. "Well, yes, one blew for many a year. But it's not needed now, not with all the fancy equipment modern vessels have."

"When did they take it out?" T.J. persisted.

Uncle Will stopped to think. "Don't know as they took it out. Just don't fire it up. They've anchored some wave-powered whistle buoys out there, of course."

Of course. But those silly whistle buoys didn't sound anything like *her* foghorn. "Uncle Will," T.J. said hesitantly, "did real foghorns ever say . . . words?"

"Words?" Uncle Will looked upset. She just bet Auntie Onion had told him she'd been hearing things! "Every horn has its own special voice and rhythm so you know which one is blowing. But

40

the message to sailors is always the same. 'Beware! Beware!' "

T.J. shivered and turned back to the spyglass. "Pigeon Point is a nice name," she said.

Uncle Will seemed glad to change the subject. He sat down in his captain's chair and pushed his hat back on his head. "Before the wreck of the *Carrier Pigeon* this was known as Whaler's Point. Spanish seamen charted this bay long before the Pilgrims ever set sight on Plymouth Rock."

"How about right now?" asked T.J. She didn't need history lessons on vacation. "Are boats still out there?"

"Fishing boats. Barges. Freighters. Tankers. Container ships. A regular water traffic jam," Uncle Will assured her, "but no more wrecks, thank fortune."

"Have you ever heard of a ship called . . ." T.J. had a sudden inspiration, "something like the *Koala*?"

"*Koala*? You mean the Australian bear?" He shook his head and drew a book from the shelf. "But speaking of Australia . . ." He flipped through the pages, stopping at a photograph of seashells. "Here's your shell, just as I said!" Uncle Will was excited all over again. "The zebra volute! 'Common to the waters of Australia's eastern shores.' "

"And I'll bet Sydney's on the eastern shore, too!" said T.J., getting excited herself.

41

"Right!" Uncle Will snapped the book shut. "Now, the question is, how did it get from there to here?"

"Maybe a gull brought it," suggested T.J.

"A seven-thousand-mile flight? Hardly. That shell's a real mystery." Uncle Will looked slyly at her. "Wouldn't mind having it myself. Add it to my collection."

T.J. walked over to the curio cabinet. She pulled on the door, but it was locked, so she had to content herself with looking through the glass. The shelves were crammed. Beside the big abalone were conch shells and scallops and sand dollars. There was a large ship's compass and glass floats from fishing nets, a carved shark's tooth and lots of rusty old nails and buttons and bits of brass that must have come from ships. A sea-green plate, decorated with thin red lines, like whirligigs, was on a stand at the back. It looked awfully old, and as delicate as Auntie Onion's teacups. Too bad a piece was broken from the rim.

"Where did you get all this stuff?" asked T.J.

Uncle Will beamed. "Found most of it myself, and right here on the beach, too. Salvage crews came in after the shipwrecks and carted off the valuables, but now and then something of interest washes up. Like your zebra shell," he added pointedly.

T.J. said, "I thought I'd put it in my aquarium."

"Well, suit yourself."

He must have learned that from Auntie Onion. Uncle Will looked disappointed, but, after all, he had a whole cabinet full of things. She had only one unusual shell.

At bedtime, T.J. put the zebra shell under her pillow. She missed having Flotsam curled up beside her. The cat had not even turned up for dinner. The shell was smooth and cool to the touch, not soft and warm like Sam. But it was comforting to have, all the same.

6

T.J. dreamed that she was climbing the rigging of a sailing ship. The ropes stretched up and up, swaying beneath her feet, making her dizzy. When she was almost to the top, she spied a head—a red head—poking from the crow's nest. It was that boy, that sailor. He pointed below, and T.J. saw hundreds of rats scrambling over the deck. They were leaving the sinking ship. Then, "Jill overboard!" the boy cried, and she was falling, down, down . . .

T.J. jerked awake, clutching her pillow. On the floor beside her bed lay the zebra shell, winking up at her. Perhaps it had caused her nightmare. She'd better put it back up on the dresser. That was just what she was intending to do when she heard a scuffling sort of sound coming from the bottom drawer. In the shadowy dawn light she could see some of the clothes she'd dumped the night before, spilling out of the half-open drawer. What if an honest-to-gosh rat was making a nest inside?

T.J. looked around for a weapon, settled on one of her slippers, and inched deliberately toward the dresser. Ready to swat, she peered in. Two round yellow eyes stared back at her.

"Sam!"

T.J. pulled the drawer wide open. It was Flot-sam, no mistake. And beside her, jumbled together, were kittens. The cat purred and licked her kittens, fluffing up their fur.

"One . . . two . . . three . . ." counted T.J. "Four! You've got quadruplets, Sam!"

The kittens were tiny, with ears flat to their heads, and inch-long tails, like little caterpillars. Their eyes were shut, and they squirmed blindly, trying to nurse. There was an orange tiger stripe and a white one with black spots and two black paws. The third was all gray, but the fourth was a calico, exactly like its mother.

"Auntie Onion!" screamed T.J., loudly enough to wake her aunt, hearing aid or not. "Come look!"

For an old lady, Auntie Onion could move very fast. "Jumping catfish!" she declared, leaning against the dresser, breathless. "Flotsam's up and had her kittens, right on your nice blue sweater!" She shook

45

her head. "Look at that drawer. It's a real rat's nest!"

Auntie Onion would not hear of leaving Flotsam and her kittens in the dresser. She fixed up what she called a cat caddy from an apple carton, lining it with an old flannel shirt of Uncle Will's. T.J.'s sweater she stuffed in her bathrobe pocket. "Needs a good wash," she said. She shook the rest of T.J.'s clothes vigorously before returning them to the drawer, leaving it open to air.

T.J. carried the box of kittens downstairs, one careful step at a time, and tucked it under the kitchen table. At first, Flotsam meowed objections and sniffed the new quarters with twitching whiskers, but after a thorough inspection, she settled down to feed her family.

Uncle Will stamped into the kitchen, complaining about such an early-morning ruckus. But T.J. could tell he was as soft as a marshmallow when it came to kittens, for he crept under the table on his hands and knees to admire them. "Look healthy to me," he pronounced, "although right now my eyes aren't much wider open than theirs are." He backed out from beneath the tablecloth. "What are you going to name them, T.J.?"

"Me?"

"Flotsam chose *your* sweater, didn't she?"

"I haven't thought about names. I don't even know if they're boys or girls."

"No hurry," Uncle Will said. "We can't be sure

about the others for a while, but it's certain that calico's a female."

"How can you tell?"

"You never see a three-colored tomcat, that's why. A calico's always a she-cat. And ever so often one pops up that's the spitting image of her ma."

"Just think!" said T.J. "Someday a whole parade of calicos will follow Sam down to the beach."

"I can't!" Auntie Onion sighed. "I can't think until I've had my coffee." She lit the burner under the pot. "And Flotsam's already given us more kittens than I can handle."

"Once this batch is weaned, Flotsam should be spayed," Uncle Will agreed.

"But . . . then could I have this calico?" asked T.J.

"I don't see how that's possible." Auntie Onion looked genuinely sorry. "The kittens will hardly have opened their eyes before you leave."

"Perhaps we could send it along later," suggested Uncle Will. "Ship it to Ohio by *Flying Tiger*!"

"I wonder . . ." Auntie Onion remarked doubtfully. She opened the refrigerator and stared inside. But she could not have been considering the kitten, for she finished ". . . if it's too early for breakfast."

"Not for me," said Uncle Will. "You can dish me up an order of Adam-and-Eve-on-a-raft."

That turned out to be two poached eggs on a piece of toast, but T.J. had something she liked even better: cereal topped with ripe red raspberries.

The calico kitten was not mentioned again, and T.J. was grateful. Not that she didn't want a kitten. If her mom would let her—and she never would— T.J. would take three. But not the calico. As soon as she'd seen it, she planned to give it to that boy. It would be second best to his lost Samantha, and first best as a thank you for the shell. T.J. was absolutely, positively certain he'd somehow slipped the zebra shell into her sweater pocket. But no way could she explain that to her aunt and uncle, since she couldn't even explain it to herself.

The morning went quickly because there were the kittens to cuddle, and by two o'clock, T.J.'s twenty-four hours of being grounded were over. The chart said the tide was low, but Auntie Onion fussed anyway and said T.J. had to be back in an hour to show "mature responsibility." T.J. promised, because an hour was better than nothing.

The sun was fully out by now, and the ocean was a brighter blue than her sweater. Auntie Onion already had that swishing around in the washing machine, but it was so warm today T.J. didn't need it. It was hard to remember how frightening the cove had seemed yesterday at high tide in the cold and fog.

T.J. walked over to the flat rock where the boy had sat. Only small ripples licked its base, flickering now and then with bits of silver whenever a wave caught a sunbeam. She stretched out on the sun-warmed boulder. It was pretty comfortable, for a rock. But even as she waited she had this notion that the boy wasn't going to come at all. Jana would say that the vibes were wrong, but T.J. felt it was more than that. If the fog was missing, then so was the foghorn, and probably the boy would be, too. It was as if all three were connected.

She sat up to watch the shorebirds scurry back and forth along the water's edge. The sandpipers moved as fast as wind-up toys on their straight stick legs, and the tracks they left behind them looked like rows of hieroglyphics. Something else was marked in the sand, up where it was drier, near the old log. T.J. went to see. There were three big letters carefully blocked out. The writer had begun to scratch a fourth and then had dropped the stick beside the unfinished word.

"Hello!" she shouted. "Are you here?"

"I'm coming!"

T.J. spun around. Sauntering up the beach was a boy. But not *the* boy. This was a little kid, not more than nine years old. Some hunk to meet on the beach!

"What did you want me for?" the boy asked.

"I don't want you for anything," T.J. answered sourly. "And I'm not supposed to talk to strangers."

"I'm not a stranger. I'm Winston D-for-Daniel Osborn and I live around here. You're the stranger."

49

"I'm visiting my aunt and uncle." T.J. waved her hand vaguely toward the house. Only the top of the Crow's Nest was visible.

"I know who they are," said Winston. "I know their cat, too. He hangs out at the beach a lot."

"He's a her," said T.J., "named Flotsam. Mine's T.J. DuMar."

The boy extended a grimy left hand, keeping the right stuffed in the pocket of his shorts. T.J. shook just the tops of his fingers, dropping them as soon as she could and still be polite. "T.J.'s short for Theresa Junior because I'm named after my mom," she explained. Winston stared glumly at her, so she added, "It's sort of a family joke."

"Ha, ha," Winston replied, not laughing. He scuffed at a shell with his bare toe.

Now it was T.J. who stared. All ten of his toes were painted a disgusting purple. The kid was wearing nail polish!

"I see you're admiring my feet," said Winston, and grinned.

"Who could miss them?" T.J. asked.

"I paint them to annoy my mother. She's afraid I'm turning punk."

"It is . . . different," said T.J.

"Want to see something else?" Winston offered. "Look!" He pulled his right hand from his pocket.

T.J. inched closer. He was holding something. "What's that?"

"A baby octopus!" He dangled it by one tentacle,

50

wiggling it back and forth. "I found it on the beach."

"Yuk!" T.J. jumped back.

"It's dead," said Winston. "I'd rather have a live cat like yours."

The octopus was very dead, limp and slimy. "Now *you* look," T.J. demanded. She pointed to the letters in the sand. "What's that supposed to mean?"

Winston gently slipped the octopus back into the pocket of his shorts and wandered over to the old log. "COY? I wouldn't write a dumb thing like that."

"Well, somebody did. And you're the only somebody I see."

He ignored her, cocking his head to one side and studying the unfinished message. "COY . . . COYA!" Winston yelled proudly. "It's an *A* that's missing."

"So?" All of a sudden T.J.'s insides knotted in a sharp cramp, as if she'd been running. Her stomach had figured it out before her head had. "Is that the name of a ship?"

"It *was* the name of a ship," Winston agreed.

"What do you mean?"

"I mean it isn't a ship anymore. The *Coya* wrecked." He jerked his thumb at the ocean. "It went down out there. Smashed to bits on the rocks."

T.J. stared down at the letters in the sand. A little yard bear like Winston didn't know everything.

But Winston seemed to think he did, because he went right on. "The *Coya* was out of Australia.

51

Most everyone aboard her drowned."

"When?"

"I don't remember exactly." For the first time he sounded uncertain. "In the sixties, I guess."

"That was over twenty years ago!"

"The *eighteen* sixties."

More than one hundred years! T.J. eyed Winston suspiciously. "Are you making this up?"

"Not me," Winston answered, insulted.

"Then how come you know so much about it?"

"Because I did a report on it, that's why. For California history. 'The Wreck of the *Coya*' by Winston D. Osborn."

"Could I read it?"

"I don't exactly carry it around with me," said Winston. "Even if I did get an A minus. How come you're so interested?"

"I . . . like history." That wasn't a lie. She was getting *very* interested.

"Okay," Winston agreed, "if I can find it." He rubbed out the letters in the sand with his big toe. Most of the polish had worn off the nail. Then he picked up the stick, drew a grid, and put an *X* in the middle. "Play you a game of tic-tac-toe," he suggested.

T.J. shook her head. "I'm already late getting back. But next time I will." If she didn't hurry, Auntie Onion would never let her have a next time. "I promise. And please bring that report you wrote."

She did hurry. At least her legs were pumping

up the path, but her mind was still back on the beach. If Winston was right, then the *Coya* sank over a century ago. So if it really was that sailor's ship, how could he still be around? T.J. did not even want to think about the answer to that.

7

T.J. was only four minutes late getting back, but she could have been forty for all anybody cared. Auntie Onion was napping and Uncle Will had stowed himself away up in the Crow's Nest. Not even Flotsam greeted her. T.J. flipped up the tablecloth and peered into the carton. It was empty!

Those kittens could not climb out of the box. They could hardly stand up. And who besides *him* would ever try to steal Sam?

It was his fault, that disappearing boy's. If it weren't for him, she wouldn't even have gone down to the beach today. She would have stayed right here with Sam and her kittens. Maybe a little bit was her fault, too. If she hadn't wasted time talking to that Winston . . . But she'd only been gone a little over an hour. Whatever could have happened?

"So, Super Sleuth," T.J. said loudly, her voice echoing in the empty kitchen, "solve the Case of the Missing Cats!"

The kitchen window was only an inch or two ajar. Not even a skinny kitten could have squeezed through it. T.J. checked under the sink, went through the cupboards, and even looked in the dishwasher. No cats. No clues. Not so much as a paw print. Thinking like a detective wasn't getting her anywhere. She had to start thinking like a cat.

If she were a mother cat with young to care for, where would she be?

Of course.

That's exactly where T.J. found Flotsam and her family. All five were once again snuggled in the bottom drawer of the dresser. Sam must have picked up each kit by the scruff of the neck and carried it through the kitchen, up the stairs, and into T.J.'s bedroom.

"Imagine!" said Auntie Onion later. "That's a lion-sized chore for a house cat, and I dozed right through it all."

Her aunt allowed that it would be foolish to take the kittens back downstairs if Flotsam was determined to haul them up, so they let them stay there. But first T.J. emptied the drawer, except for her blue sweater. When Auntie Onion had washed it, she'd used hot water and a generous dose of bleach.

Then she'd put the sweater in the dryer. Now it was doll sized and foggy colored, like the little gray kitty. Maybe that would be a good name for the kitten. Foggy. Flotsam turned round and round on the sweater, kneading it with her toes before she finally rumbled approval and bedded down beside her litter.

Auntie Onion found T.J. another carton for the rest of her clothes. That worked out quite well. At bedtime, T.J. didn't have to put anything away. She just tossed what she'd been wearing into the box and dug out her pajamas. She had plenty of company, too, all night long. Once when she awakened to pull up the blanket, she heard a kitten mewing. And then she did not hear anything more until the foghorn called her in the morning.

Her eyes popped open as soon as she heard that low, insistent "Tee-Jay-a-ay!" Did it call him, too? She bolted out of bed and into her clothes. She wasn't going to miss seeing that boy if she could help it. She had some questions to ask him, important questions that even a know-it-all kid like Winston couldn't answer.

T.J. did not realize how early it was until she got down to the kitchen. The clock said only six forty-five. No one else was awake. Uncle Will's snores whistled down the stairway. No wonder Auntie Onion never wore her hearing aid to bed.

T.J. checked the tide table. Lowest water had been at six thirty, just a few minutes ago. She penciled "The tide has gone out and so have I" on a piece of paper, adding, "Back soon." She stuck the note on the spout of the coffeepot where Auntie Onion would see it first thing, grabbed a few graham crackers, and tiptoed out the door.

The fog was thin this morning. Already the sun shone through the haze like a flashlight's beam through tissue paper. The boy said that the foghorn only blew in a special spell of fog. If the sky turned really sunny, it wouldn't call again. The boy wouldn't come, and she wouldn't find out who or what he was. She'd be left just as curious as ever.

As soon as she reached the beach, she saw him, sitting on the rock, waiting. He saw her, too. The boy held a hollow length of kelp up to one eye, pretending it was a spyglass, and focused right on her. T.J. stopped. Curiosity had killed a cat.

The boy beckoned. "Pipe you aboard, Miss!" he called. He put the strand of kelp to his mouth, puffed out his cheeks, and blew. The kelp squawked like a rooster with a bad cold.

No one could be afraid of anyone so silly! T.J. cleared her throat. "I came to thank you for the shell," she said. "The one you put in the pocket of my sweater."

"Now whatever makes you think 'twas me?"

"No one else was here." T.J. wanted to add that she wasn't sure he'd actually been there either, but instead she blurted, "And COYA! You wrote that, too. That was the name of your ship."

"Aye. I told you so."

"Yes, but this little kid said the *Coya* wrecked years and years ago."

" 'Aye' to that as well."

Apparently he was just going to sit there and wave that old seaweed and let her struggle. T.J. scuffed a foot back and forth in the sand. "Did everyone aboard the *Coya* . . . go overboard?"

"Three mates got to shore."

"One was you!" T.J. cried. "Because you're here now."

"I'm here because the foghorn bids me come," he answered, adding, "same as it does to you."

"But I'm real and you're . . ." T.J. gulped.

"Not?" He held out his pale arm and drops of water splashed onto the rock. "Would you like to pinch me and find out?"

"No," whispered T.J. There wasn't any need to. She'd guessed. She was talking to a dripping wet, dead-and-drowned ghost! "Do you know why the foghorn calls you?"

"It bids me seek my ring. Strange it should break its silence now. I never heard its voice until you came."

"I don't see what I have to do with it," said T.J. "Is your ring terribly important?"

" 'Tis my gold wedding band."

Married! That was too much to believe. He wasn't old enough, not even if he had been around for a hundred and thirty years. "You couldn't have a wife!" T.J. declared.

"Wife!" He looked just as surprised as T.J. "Why should a lad like me take on a storm-and-strife?"

"Huh?"

"Storm-and-strife. Wife."

"I don't speak Australian," said T.J.

"No," he answered scornfully. "The likes of you'd know nothing of rhyming slang." He suddenly leaned closer and blew again on his kelp pipe. This time the sound was low and spooky. A moan.

T.J. jumped back. "Maybe I know enough already," she said hoarsely.

"Don't leave! I've not had anyone to talk to for a whale's age." He shifted the kelp to his left hand and held up his right, like someone taking a pledge. "I'll not frighten you again. And I'll teach you rhyming slang, if you like."

Slang? From a ghost? "Not me," said T.J. She had enough trouble understanding him without having to figure out jingles.

"You just talk in rhymes and use one word to take the place of another," he explained. "Listen! Eyes." He blinked. "Apple pies!" He laid a finger beside his nose. "This is my ruby rose." Then he raised the kelp like an ear trumpet. "Ears are tears-and-cheers."

"I don't get it." T.J. shook her head. "And I don't get the point."

59

"That *is* the point!" he said triumphantly. "It's hard to understand at first. That's why you use two words instead of just one and sometimes only rhyme the last. Thieves and robbers and the like invented it in London so's they could outwit any eaves-droppers."

"A secret code!" T.J. caught her breath. Wouldn't Jana simply die when she heard it! "Teach me!" she begged him.

"Well," he said, looking at her thoughtfully, "I see there's some seaweed on your uncles-and-aunts."

T.J. was stumped. She scraped her shoe back and forth in the sand. A twist of green weed clung to the hem of her jeans. "I know!" she shouted. "Pants!"

"Right you are. Now you give it a go."

T.J. thought for a moment and asked, "Samantha. Was she the ship's mouse-and-rat?"

"The ship's cat!" He tapped the top of her head with the kelp. "Soon you will be sounding like a true Jack-tar. Near all of us speak rhyming slang."

It seemed to T.J. that he was even more pleased with himself than with her. He acted like he'd taught some dumb parrot how to ask for a cracker. "So what happened to Samantha?" Perhaps a ghost boy could have a ghost cat.

"I cannot say for certain," he answered, all cockiness gone from his voice. "Though it is tradition of the sea to save the ship's cat first."

"You don't believe she did drown! That's why you mistook Flotsam for her." She wasn't so dumb.

"I was addled the day we met," he said, shrugging. "How could the creature still be hereabouts, if she'd gotten to shore at all?"

"Maybe she did! Maybe her great-great-great-great-great"—T.J. was running out of *greats*—"granddaughter is here right now!"

"I have my doubts of that."

"I don't!" T.J. hopped up and down, kicking up spurts of sand. "Because Flotsam's had her kittens, and one of them is a calico, exactly like her. And like your Samantha. And you can have this one if you want."

"Thanks to you for thinking of me," he said softly. "I'm obliged to take but one thing along with me, and that is my ring."

She'd forgotten all about that ring. For a moment she'd almost forgotten what he was. Of course he could not have an ordinary live kitten, ever again. "Take along? Where are you going?"

"Once I've the ring again, there'll be naught to keep me anchored here. But where? I'll wager the Lord Mayor himself cannot answer that. So why fuss and flurry?"

"Worry!"

"Aren't you clever, Miss Theresa!" he cried, jumping up. "But schooling's over." He squinted at the clearing sky. "Time I bid ta ta."

"Ta ta?" asked T.J.

She got no answer. A shaft of sunlight fell upon the boy's red head, polishing it like a new copper penny. But that was not why she stared. He cast no shadow on the rock. The sunbeams seemed to pass right through him. He was there, and yet he wasn't, and the outline of his body began to blur. The harder T.J. strained to see him, the less distinct he became. It was like trying to look at someone through eyes filled with tears.

T.J. heard a splash and ran to the rock. The water was as clear as in her aquarium, and she could see the length of kelp lying on the sandy bottom of the ocean. But the boy was not there.

She walked along the shore, chewing a graham cracker thoughtfully. He'd simply disappeared, like the first time she'd seen him. There wasn't a trace of a ghost, or the ghost of a trace. The tide was still out quite far, and rocks that T.J. had never noticed before stuck up through the surf like a giant's stepping stones. The rocks close by, the familiar ones, were well above the waterline, quite dry, the mossy seaweed stiff with salt.

T.J. crumbled the rest of her crackers for the birds and climbed up on the flat boulder. It was slippery underfoot. T.J. looked down, and a shiver danced along her spine. Where the boy had sat, drops of seawater glistened, evaporating quickly in the warm sun.

8

When T.J. returned, Auntie Onion and Uncle Will were at the kitchen table, reading the morning paper.

"Morning!" boomed Uncle Will, waving his newspaper. "And what did your sharp young eyes spy today?"

"Spy?" croaked T.J., rubbing her cheek. Perhaps she was pale, like she'd seen a ghost.

"Minus tide. Fine morning. Surely you found something on the beach?"

All he could think about was shells! "I forgot to look," T.J. mumbled.

"Forgot!" Uncle Will rustled the paper loudly and turned to the sports page.

"*Forgot*," murmured Auntie Onion, "is a common English word meaning T.J. had more important things on her mind than your curios." She looked up from the crossword puzzle and pointed her pencil at T.J. "Are you hungry, child?"

"Not very," T.J. answered. She had a queasy feeling, as if she were seasick. Or getting the flu.

"Have an orange anyway. Six letters in orange. Seven, if you count the vitamin C."

T.J. found an orange in the refrigerator, sat down, and began to peel it. Uncle Will was muttering under his breath about the Dodgers, and Auntie Onion frowned over the crossword. Neither one took notice of T.J. until she said, "Does anybody here believe in ghosts?" Then both heads snapped up.

"Ghosts!" Uncle Will snorted. "First it's foghorns, now it's ghosts! Whoever puts such nonsense in your head?"

"I was talking to that boy I'd met before, in the fog."

" 'One misty, moisty morning, when foggy was the weather, I chanced to meet an old man, clothed all in leather,' " quoted Uncle Will.

Leather! Now Auntie Onion would worry that the boy belonged to a motorcycle gang! "And then the sun came out and he disappeared," T.J. persisted.

"Practical answer for that, at least," Uncle Will reasoned. "Fog plays tricks on the eyes. Reflection, refraction, mirages . . . things you wouldn't understand."

"Well, I don't know," Auntie Onion said suddenly. "I just don't know but what I do believe in ghosts."

"Really?" asked T.J.

Auntie Onion took off her glasses and straightened a stem. When she returned them to her narrow nose, they tilted more dangerously than ever. "I certainly believe in memories," she said. "And, if you think about it, today's memories are ghosts of what was real yesterday."

That wasn't the answer T.J. wanted, but it was better than nothing. She ate her orange and had two pieces of cinnamon toast. Maybe that funny feeling in her stomach had been hunger.

T.J. wrote down *storm-and-strife* and *uncles-and-aunts* on her word list. Rhyming slang was great. No way that she and Jana could have thought up such a neat secret code. And that ghost boy had as much as admitted he'd slipped the zebra shell into her sweater pocket. But other things she was going to have to figure out by herself.

Auntie Onion and Uncle Will didn't even hear the foghorn. Weren't they special enough? Or was it because they didn't believe in it, or in ghosts either? T.J. wasn't sure she wanted to believe in ghosts herself, but she didn't have any doubts about the foghorn anymore. She had heard it, all right.

Even if she wasn't special herself, it must have a special reason for calling her. T.J. was sure it had

65

something to do with the ghost boy, but what really confused her was why *she* wanted anything to do with him. She freaked out watching spooky shows on T.V., even though bodies floating up from gravestones and falling out of closets weren't much scarier than the commercials. But this . . .

T.J. drummed her fingers against the headboard of her bed. She didn't have to see him again. If the foghorn called at night, she could pull the covers over her head. Daytimes she could wait for the fog to lift before going down to the beach. But she sort of liked the ghost boy. It wasn't anything like Jana's dumb crush on Dave; she just felt sorry for him, that's all. Maybe she was afraid, too, but in a tingly, exciting way.

She couldn't turn him off like the television. Why shouldn't she help him look for his ring? It would be like doing homework for her mystery book. And Jana could never claim to know a genuine haunt.

T.J. wished she knew his name.

"I've been thinking about names," T.J. said after dinner that night. "I was going to call that gray kitten Foggy. But Misty sounds better."

"Appropriate," Auntie Onion approved, "and kittenish."

"Misty it is," agreed Uncle Will. "One down and three to go."

They tried out some other names: Splotch for

66

the black-and-white kitten, Tiger for the striped, Sailor for the calico, but none seemed exactly right.

"You can decide later," Auntie Onion assured T.J. "After all, you'll be here for another week."

A few days ago, the time would have stretched forever. Now it seemed much too short.

T.J. went up to her room to make sure that everyone had settled in for the night. Her mom always said she kept her room like a zoo, but now there was good reason, since she was head kitten keeper. Sam was not there, but Auntie Onion had explained that every cat left her litter now and then. She always came back for the next feeding, as if there were a tiny time clock ticking inside a furry ear. With their eyes closed, it was hard to tell if the kittens were asleep or awake. T.J. hoped they would open their eyes before she had to go home.

When she went down the hall to brush her teeth, T.J. could hear Auntie Onion and Uncle Will talking. Her aunt must have hung up her hearing aid already, for their voices were raised.

"Hallucinations!" said Uncle Will. "Not normal."

"Imagination. Perfectly normal." That was Auntie Onion.

"I certainly did not go around making up people when I was a child," Uncle Will announced.

"More's the pity," replied Auntie Onion. "I did. I had a make-believe friend for quite a while."

"Boy or girl?" Uncle Will sounded suspicious.

"A unicorn. Imaginary animals make the best imaginary friends. I was lonesome, I suppose."

"T.J.'s lonely, too. That figures! A couple of old coots and a handful of felines aren't very good company."

Auntie Onion must have nodded, for T.J. did not hear a reply. Then there was a loud snap of fingers, and Uncle Will exlaimed, "Take her on an outing! The Boardwalk at Santa Cruz."

"The Giant Dipper!" Auntie Onion sighed. "Oh, how I loved that wooden roller coaster when I was young."

"Any girl would." Uncle Will chuckled. "Whatever her age."

Any girl but T.J. She rinsed out her mouth and spit into the sink. So little time, and now they planned to waste it, sending her around in circles on some rickety roller coaster.

9

"Tee-Jay-a-ay!"

T.J. stuffed her head under her pillow. That wasn't the foghorn calling. It was Auntie Onion.

"T.J.!" The voice rose sharply. "Time for breakfast!"

It was a command, not an invitation. T.J. stretched and then groped under the bed for her slippers. She supposed she had to go down and face another bowl of cereal.

"Surprise!" Auntie Onion exclaimed the moment T.J. appeared in the doorway. "Something wonderful is in store for you today."

"Cornflakes?" suggested T.J., spotting a brand-new box on the counter.

"An adventure!" Auntie Onion waggled her finger. "What and where is for me to know and you to find out."

T.J. had found out what and where and why besides, last night. But she wouldn't be mean and spoil an old lady's fun. "Is that why you're dressed up?"

Auntie Onion nodded, pleased, and smoothed her clean white dress. She had tied a yellow bandanna about her head, pirate style, covering all but a few strands of gray hair. Uncle Will sat at the kitchen table, still in his bathrobe.

"Aren't you going?" asked T.J.

"Can't." Uncle Will shook his head. "Or won't. I get seasick on roller . . ." He stopped and glanced sheepishly at Auntie Onion.

"What he means is someone else is coming along instead," she said quickly. "That boy you met on the beach."

T.J. half choked on her orange juice. "Who?"

"When I talked to his mother this morning she said he'd already met you. Nice little boy, that Quentin Osborn."

T.J. swallowed and flooded her cornflakes with milk.

"If I had known it was that Wilfred you'd been talking to . . ." Auntie Onion continued.

"Winston," T.J. interrupted.

". . . I'd not have been concerned. I'm pleased you found a chum."

Chum! T.J. sighed into her bowl.

70

"Now finish your breakfast while I see to our lunch," said her aunt.

Auntie Onion polished three apples. Then she constructed three sandwiches, thick as bricks, with cheddar cheese and onion rings between two slices of bread, mortared together with generous amounts of mustard and mayonnaise. When she'd finished, her white dress was polka-dotted with yellow.

"No need to wear anything fancy," she said to T.J. "Just find something decent."

"Umm," agreed T.J., craning her neck to peer over the top of Uncle Will's paper and see out the window. Another misty, moisty morning. But the fog did not seem very thick. Perhaps it wouldn't have been good ghost-hunting weather after all. Or rather not good weather to help a ghost in his hunting, or . . .

"Skedaddle!" Auntie Onion shouted in her ear, as if T.J. were the one who was hard of hearing.

T.J. took the last few drops of milk in her bowl up to Flotsam and dug a shirt and almost-clean shorts from the carton. Then she returned to the kitchen for Auntie Onion's inspection.

"You'll do," her aunt decided, "except for your hair."

"What's wrong with my hair?" demanded T.J. She had tried to straighten her part. "It's a new permanent."

"Permanent frizz," sniffed Auntie Onion, "at least in this salt air." She picked up a couple of bright-

71

blue rubber bands from the windowsill and grabbed a handful of T.J.'s hair.

"Ouch!"

"Hold still or you'll have rubber bands for earrings."

Auntie Onion managed to separate T.J.'s snarls into two reasonably even sections, each secured by one of the blue elastics. T.J. checked her reflection in the glass of the kitchen door. A hairy horn stuck out behind each ear.

"Hysterical!" That's exactly what Jana would say.

"Yes, practical," agreed her aunt, "especially when the wind blows."

T.J. gave up. Fog or sun, willing or no, she was off to Santa Cruz.

Uncle Will had fired up the old car and parked it in the driveway. A thundercloud of exhaust mingled with the mist. T.J. walked around the car, eyeing it critically. She had ridden in it from the airport, but she hadn't paid much attention, other than to notice that its paint was pistachio ice cream green.

"Got this car when your ma was no older than you are right now," Uncle Will said. "A 1952 DeSoto is a classic."

"Neat," T.J. murmured.

"Elbow grease," her uncle boasted. "That's my secret polish."

Auntie Onion came out, carrying a thermos, the

picnic basket, and an afghan. An enormous handbag was slung over her shoulder. She'd packed for
a month's safari, or else she was afraid that Mister
DeSoto's automobile would break down and they'd
be stranded on the beach, like castaways.

"Hop in," said Uncle Will, opening the back
door for T.J. "And hold on!"

Auntie Onion climbed in up front and gunned
the engine. The brake was still set, but T.J. hunk-
ered down and tightened her seat belt.

"Look out for your aunt," called Uncle Will,
with a wave. "She can get lost in an elevator."

"Balderdash!" Auntie Onion snorted, released
the brake, and the DeSoto took off like a huge and
dizzy grasshopper, lurching from side to side down
the driveway and nicking the mailbox as it passed.

Once on the highway, Auntie Onion eased her
tennis shoe from the accelerator and straddled the
white line down the middle of the road, going no
more than twenty miles an hour. Trucks zoomed
past, blowing their air horns, and even a bicycle
wheeled by. It seemed a dinosaur age before they
reached the Osborn house.

If T.J. had not known already, she would have
guessed their destination as soon as Winston settled
down next to her in the backseat.

"You'll freak out on that roller coaster," he announced. "Everything on the Boardwalk's cool."

"Cool!" Auntie Onion shook her head at Winston in the rearview mirror and plunged her foot

down on the gas pedal. "In my day it was hot stuff!" She would have said more, clearly annoyed that he'd let the cat out of the bag, if a jackrabbit had not suddenly jumped in front of them. She missed it by an ear, but after that Auntie Onion kept two eyes on the road, both hands on the steering wheel, and her toe at the ready on the brake.

"Do you have it?" T.J. whispered to Winston.

"I thought your aunt was bringing the lunch."

"The report! What you wrote about the *Coya*."

"I couldn't find it."

"Shoot!" said T.J. The one she wanted to shoot was Winston. She'd really counted on reading that report.

"But I did find the newspaper I used to write it. Mine was lots better than this. I drew pictures of ships and sharks and . . ."

"Let's see it," T.J. demanded.

Winston searched his pockets, pulling out a compass, a small notepad, a pencil, and a Mexican peso before he produced a faded sheet of newspaper. It was folded into triangles, as if he'd been trying to make an origami bird.

"Thanks," said T.J., slipping it into her own pocket.

"Aren't you going to read it?" Winston asked.

She was dying to. But not now. Not here, with Winston hanging over her shoulder and Auntie Onion listening to every word. "It's too bouncy in

74

the car to read," she said. "Let's play tic-tac-toe instead, like I promised."

"Me first!"

Winston dug out the notepad and pencil again and drew a grid with an *X* in the middle. T.J. put an *O* alongside and matched each of his next four marks with one of her own, so that both were dead-ended and neither won. They played five more games that way, Winston always dibbing first chance and claiming the prime middle square. In the sixth game, T.J. let him get three *X*'s in a diagonal.

"You're the champ!" she announced, and hurriedly closed the notebook before Winston could suggest Hangman or some other game.

T.J. looked out the window. Highway 1 stretched smooth and wide along the coastal headlands. Even Auntie Onion could have no trouble keeping the DeSoto plugging along in the right direction, and she hummed as she drove. Orange-streaked cliffs rose steeply on one side of the road; on the other was the ocean. Out there in the Pacific somewhere was Hawaii. T.J. tried to imagine her mom in a hula skirt. Grass made Dad sneeze.

Something was making her own nose tickle. Not grass. T.J. sniffed. "I smell onions!" she declared.

"Can't be the sandwiches," said Auntie Onion. "They're in the trunk."

T.J. tugged on one of her pigtails and swished it beneath her nose. "Yuk!" She knew now where her aunt had gotten those blue rubber bands. Before they'd been snapped about her hair, those bands had held together fat bunches of green onions.

The DeSoto snorted slowly up a rise, rested for a moment at the top, and then began to coast down the other side of the hill. They left the last shreds of mist behind them, and by the time they reached the beach at Santa Cruz, the sun was shining brightly on the bay, on the sand, and upon hundreds of glistening bodies.

"What a pity!" said Auntie Onion, shaking out the old knit afghan and squeezing it between a couple of striped towels and a beach umbrella. "If I had known it would be such a nice day, we'd have brought along our swimsuits."

T.J. was glad that her own striped bathing suit was buried somewhere at the bottom of the carton. It made her look like a candy cane. And she could just imagine what Auntie Onion's bathing get-up was like. It probably had a skirt, with bloomers.

"I wore mine," Winston informed them, peeling off his clothes. He was wearing ordinary tan swim trunks, but his toenails flashed like pink neon lights. Now Auntie Onion was taking off her socks and shoes, too, and hiking up her dress, tucking it into her belt so that it swung well above her knotted knees.

"At least we can wade," she said to T.J. "The surf's safe here at Santa Cruz."

"I'll just watch," whispered T.J. Why not? Everyone within fifty feet was watching.

"Last one in is a rubber chicken!" cried Auntie Onion. She and Winston raced toward the blue Pacific, hopping across towels and over beach bags, showering sand as they ran.

T.J. flopped back on the afghan and pretended she'd never seen either one of them before. When it was safe, when she was certain they were out of sight, she sat up and pulled out the newspaper clipping.

It was old, all right. The print was practically rubbed off along the creases. But not as old as she had hoped. She had thought it might go all the way back to when it happened, when the *Coya* went down. But the date at the top said "May 12, 1968." It looked more like a magazine story than a newspaper. Perhaps it was a feature from the Sunday section. She read aloud:

"SHIPWRECKS OF YESTERYEAR
In the summer of 1866, the *Coya* set sail from Sydney, Australia, bound for San Francisco. The ship was British, a three-masted, square-rigged barque."

Barque. That threw her, but she had seen that word before somewhere. "Bark!" exclaimed T.J. That's how you said it. "Bark!"

A boy two towels over gave her a peculiar look, so she read the rest of the paragraph to herself.

The cargo was coal, but there were a few pieces of Chinese porcelain and ivory in the hold as well. The *Coya* plowed a steady course across the vast Pacific, and then, almost within sight of her destination, she sank. The reason was fog.

Fog. T.J. shivered, despite the sun, and buried her feet in the warm sand.

For two days, the crew of the *Coya* steered through coastal mist as thick as wool. Forced to sail by dead reckoning, they believed the ship to be yet miles offshore. Then, shortly after midnight of the third day, the watch in the crow's nest saw a crest of white foam against the dark of the sea. Breakers!

"Hard to starboard!" he shouted, but before anyone could spin the tiller, the *Coya* smashed against the reef, turned broadside, and rolled over in deep water. The barque sank almost at once, taking nearly everyone aboard with her.

T.J. shaded her eyes and looked out at the Pacific, calm as a blue-green puddle now. She saw her aunt splashing at the water's edge, getting her dress all wet. Then she caught sight of Winston, belly-slamming on a wave. The two of them were certainly having fun without her, and she'd thought the whole idea of this trip was to keep her from being lonesome. Okay for them. She had better things to do. She lay back again, propping her chin in her hand and her feet on the picnic basket.

Only three survived. They had lashed themselves to pieces of wreckage and were finally washed
ashore. One was a passenger, George Burns. One
was a mate, Thomas Bearstow. The third was the
ship's cabin boy, Walter Cooper.

Walter Cooper! The ship's cabin boy. "Him!"
said T.J. softly.

Among the drowned were Captain Paige, his
wife, and their five-year-old daughter. It was ru-
mored that the losses also included a thirteen-year-
old stov—

The rest of the sentence had disappeared into
the crease, wrinkled and unreadable, but the story
continued on the other side. T.J. had just flipped
the paper over when a shower of drops fell on her
head.

Winston was shaking himself like a water span-
iel. Auntie Onion was rubbing the salt from her
legs with her bandanna. They'd sneaked up on her
as quietly as—as ghosts! Reluctantly T.J. refolded
the page and slipped it back into her pocket.

"Too bad you didn't join us," said Auntie Onion
cheerfully, spreading out the lunch.

The thermos held cool lemonade, and the apples, although warm to the touch, were crisp and
crunchy. The sandwiches were crunchy, too.

"Ugh!" Winston made a face. "A sand sand-
wich."

When he was sure that Auntie Onion was not looking and that T.J. was, he tossed an onion ring into the air. The onion sailed like a Frisbee and brushed a low-flying gull.

"Gull's-eye!" crowed Winston. "How about that!"

10

Auntie Onion stashed the hamper and blanket in the trunk, slammed the lid, and ordered a march to the Boardwalk.

"Giant Dipper first," she said firmly. "Best roller in the west."

"I'll bet T.J.'s scared." Winston smirked. "She was even afraid to go in the ocean."

T.J. stared at the enormous wooden structure towering over the Boardwalk. From below, it looked like a big Tinker Toy. "I'm not scared," she retorted. "Not of the ocean, or of that thing, either."

"Prove it," Winston dared her.

So she had to.

T.J. and Winston shared the front of the coaster car and Auntie Onion claimed the rear for herself, sitting stiff and tall as a queen in a chariot. A sign read, "Keep your seat!"

The car rattled through a dark tunnel and then jerked up a long, steep grade. At the top it teetered for a moment and, with a whoosh, began its downward slide. Not all of T.J. was going down. Her pigtails were flying straight out to the sides, and it felt like she had left her stomach far behind. They went up once more, hugged a curve, and then up, around, and down again. Each twist hit T.J. with a wallop. She was not sure she could keep her seat, or anything else. Someone screamed, and she thought it was Winston, but it might have been T.J. herself. Then she heard Auntie Onion. Holding on tight, T.J. peered over her shoulder. Her aunt was flapping her yellow bandanna, her gray hair was blowing, and her mouth was opened wide. But that whoop wasn't a scream. Auntie Onion was laughing.

"Razzmatazz!" declared Auntie Onion when they got off.

"Super!" Winston's voice was a croak.

Although T.J.'s shirt had come untucked, the rubber bands had kept her hair from escaping. She grinned at her aunt. "I thought high places gave you vertigo."

"They do. But the worse I feel, the better the ride."

T.J. knew exactly what she meant. Being scared

was half the fun, although she wasn't about to admit that to Winston.

"Now for the merry-go-round!" cried Auntie Onion.

From scary to sissy, thought T.J. She'd outgrown merry-go-rounds a long time ago. But Auntie Onion had already hurried ahead to the brightly painted carousel and was buying tickets.

"Look!" she declared. "All sixty-two of these animals were carved by hand." She reached out to pat a wooden horse. "Seventy-seven years ago and still going strong!"

"Like your aunt," Winston whispered, as he climbed up on a palomino.

Auntie Onion was already perched sidesaddle on a high-stepping bay, so T.J. resigned herself to a spotted pony. She'd tell Jana she had a ride on an Appaloosa out west.

Music burst from the pipe organ and the horses began to circle. As the music swelled, the merry-go-round twirled faster. Auntie Onion bounced up and down, holding tight to the pole, and shouted over the noise, "Try for the brass ring!"

Both T.J. and Winston missed the ring as they sped past. He looked disgusted, but T.J. did not really care. The shiny brass ring was only good for a free ride. The idea it gave her was worth a lot more.

Auntie Onion had to be a mind reader, for, as

soon as they had dismounted, she opened her large purse and produced two five-dollar bills. "For whatever you want," she said, handing one to Winston and the other to T.J.

What Winston wanted was a chocolate-covered banana, but, "No, thanks," said T.J. "I'm spending this money on a special souvenir."

"Suit yourself," said Auntie Onion, plopping down on a bench. She opened her handbag again, but this time she pulled out her crocheting. "I've had enough thrills for one day. You two enjoy yourselves, but keep an eye on one another."

T.J. was glad to see Auntie Onion finally acting her age. She waved good-bye to her and followed Winston into the arcade. It was like walking into a cave, only instead of stalagmites rising up from the floor, there were electronic whiz-bang machines. Winston played a couple of them, but T.J. knew she wouldn't find what she wanted in a place like this.

She drifted out onto the Boardwalk again. A million people elbowed each other and the music, carnival and country western, was loud enough for her folks to hear clear over in Hawaii. T.J. ducked into a souvenir shop. The store was jammed to the ceiling with pennants and hats, fuzzy stuffed animals, and T-shirts that boasted, "Never Bored on the Boardwalk."

"Just looking," said T.J. She'd certainly not find it here, either.

She saw Winston as soon as she came out. He was just swallowing the last bit of fluff from a cone of cotton candy before climbing aboard a ride called The Spider. The cars were painted to look like tarantulas, and the track was as twisted as a spiderweb. Just watching it made her head whirl. She went over to The Haunted House instead, but she didn't buy a ticket. She could get spooked in her great-aunt's place for nothing.

A shop with necklaces in the window caught her eye and T.J. hurried in. She inspected the case of rings, each studded with a big bright jewel. Fake. "Do you have any plain rings?" she asked.

The lady behind the counter raised her eyebrows. "Well, we have a silver friendship ring, just right for a young girl . . ."

"No," said T.J. "The ring I need has to be gold." She put her five-dollar bill on top of the glass case.

The woman pushed it away. "Better start saving your allowance then, sweetie. Nothing here goes for less than ten dollars."

Ten dollars! Not much chance of digging that much up, unless she found buried treasure. T.J. pulled the door shut behind her and looked for Winston. He was no longer spinning around on The Spider. She didn't see him in line for any of the other rides, either, or standing at one of the booths. Keeping an eye on that pest was a job for the FBI. T.J. was about to go tell Auntie Onion that she'd lost him when she remembered The Sky

Glider. The baskets bobbed along slowly, one hundred feet overhead, for the entire length of the Boardwalk. From up there, she'd have a bird's-eye view of everything. And everyone. Reluctantly, T.J. handed her five-dollar bill to the man selling tickets. He gave her four crumpled one-dollar bills and two quarters in return and pointed toward one of the baskets.

The Glider was about as exciting as a ride in a baby buggy, and trying to find Winston in the jam of people below was worse than sorting out a jigsaw puzzle. Then, at the far end of the Boardwalk, T.J. spotted a boy leaning on a trash can and squirting mustard on a hot dog.

"Winston!" T.J. shouted.

He looked up, waved the hot dog, and yelled back, "Some fun, huh?"

Fun! When she caught up with him, T.J. was mad enough to hang him from The Sky Glider. Without a basket.

"Hi!" said Winston cheerfully, licking the mustard from his fingers. "Will you loan me fifty cents?"

"You just cost me that much," T.J. began.

"You've got lots more money," Winston protested. "And you owe me a favor for bringing you that old paper. You're lucky my dad saves stuff like that."

T.J. fingered the two quarters.

"Stingy!"

She handed the coins to Winston, and he dashed over to wait in line for something called The Rip Tide.

T.J. walked back to Auntie Onion and slumped beside her on the bench.

"Tired?" asked her aunt.

"Sort of," T.J. replied. "I couldn't get what I wanted."

Auntie Onion looked surprised. "There must be something you like in all this."

T.J. didn't answer. She watched as Winston careened about on The Rip Tide. The cars lurched around the corners on two wheels. When it was over, Winston wobbled toward them and asked, "What next?"

"Not much next." Auntie Onion squinted at her watch. "It's almost time to go." She put her crocheting away. "Don't be so picky," she told T.J. "Hurry and get your souvenir."

T.J. crossed the sidewalk to a small booth that sold buttons and bumper stickers. One of them read, "Honk if you're from Alabama." There were stickers for most of the other states, too. T.J. riffled through the pile. Wouldn't Dave have a blast with "Honk if you're from Ohio" pasted on his car? Everyone in Cleveland would blow their horns as he drove by.

Although the strip was only paper, it cost T.J. two dollars and fifteen cents, with tax.

"That's highway robbery!" said Auntie Onion, clucking her tongue as she tucked the sticker into her bulging purse.

Next door was one of those test-your-skill stalls. Fat-necked bottles were lined up on shelves, just like at a grocery store, only these bottles were empty. A pile of red plastic rings lay on the counter.

"Ring the bottle!" coaxed the man in the booth. He was dressed as a clown, with a painted-on smile. "Five tries for a dollar. Three ringers win a valuable prize!"

It looked pretty easy. If Winston could hit a gull in midair, she could certainly collar a standing-still bottle. T.J. put down a dollar and picked up five rings.

The rings were light and slightly lopsided, and T.J.'s first try fell short. Her second and third pitches were better, but the rings bounced off the targets as if they had springs. The fourth quavered for a moment and then settled about the glass neck, but her fifth toss was too hard and too high.

"Play again, little lady," urged the clown.

T.J. dug the remaining eighty-five cents from her pocket. "I'm a little bit short," she apologized.

The man scowled above his smiley mouth. Then Auntie Onion stepped up beside T.J. and plunked down a dime and a nickel. "Go ahead, T.J.," she said, glaring at the man.

T.J. studied the bottles and licked her lips. She threw carefully and ringed a bottle with the very first toss. The second ring veered to the right, but she got a ringer with the third. Her hand shook as she threw the fourth ring and her aim was terrible.

"Hold on!" said Auntie Onion. "My fifteen cents should buy me a turn, too." She helped herself to the last ring and twirled it in her fingers. "Flimsy!"

Auntie Onion adjusted her glasses, leaned to one side, and tossed with a twist of her wrist. The ring spiraled into the air, ricocheted off the plywood ceiling, and came to rest neatly around a bottle.

"Wow!" yelled Winston.

Auntie Onion dusted her hands on her dress and turned to T.J. "Pick your prize," she said.

T.J. was trying to decide between a stuffed green parrot on a stick and a plastic kitten bank that nodded its head when she saw the rings. Rings to wear, not throw. The tray was almost hidden from sight beneath an array of parrot feathers, but there, unmistakably, in the third row, gleamed a circle of gold.

"I'd like that gold ring," said T.J. firmly.

"A ring!" Winston snorted. "That's a dumb souvenir."

"Your sister's smart," said the man hastily, thrusting the ring at T.J. He seemed to want to get rid of them before Auntie Onion played again. "This ring is chock full of carats."

"She's not my sister . . . ," Winston began.

"Carrots!" Auntie Onion interrupted. "My land, if we don't hurry, we'll be late for dinner!"

As they drove home, T.J. held the ring at arm's length so as to catch the slanting beams from the afternoon sun. Except for the "Santa Cruz, California" written around the band, it was perfect. "Wonderful!" she said to Auntie Onion.

"A wonderful day," agreed her aunt. "Every fifty years I'm going to ride a roller coaster." She accelerated sharply around a bend.

Winston didn't say anything. All of a sudden he turned as green as the DeSoto. He clapped one hand over his mouth and waved wildly with the other. Auntie Onion pulled to the side of the road and Winston darted into the bushes.

"Heavens to Hannah!" cried Auntie Onion. "Do you suppose it was the sandwiches?"

11

Over dinner, Uncle Will had to hear all the little details of their day, down to the last crumb. He admired T.J.'s ring but did not seem surprised that Auntie Onion had made the winning throw.

"In seventh grade your aunt Elizabeth was the best basketball player in the whole junior high. Of course, she stretched up a head taller than anyone else, except maybe the chemistry teacher." Auntie Onion snorted and he patted her hand. "I guess she hasn't lost her touch in sixty years."

T.J. nodded but did not look up. She hoped they'd think she was concentrating on her ring, but really she was counting on her fingers. Auntie Onion would have been twelve or thirteen in the seventh grade. Add sixty. That certainly made her aunt great enough. Seventy-two, going on seventy-three.

"Now hear this!" said Uncle Will, tapping his fork against his water glass to get T.J.'s attention. "I'd planned on tending to duty today . . ."

"Flat on your back and snoring," interrupted Auntie Onion.

". . . and I was headed for the Crow's Nest," he continued, ignoring her, "when I perceived a peculiar noise coming from T.J.'s room. Cross between a whimper and a squawk. 'That's an S.O.S. call,' said I to myself, so in I went, full speed ahead. In the middle of the floor I saw this kitten. It was the tiger stripe, and how it got out of the drawer I don't know. He was going around in circles, tail up straight as a mizzenmast, and piping to beat the band."

"The tiger's eyes are open!" exclaimed T.J.

"Nope. Still battened shut. That kitten was navigating by dead reckoning."

It was the second time today she'd come across those words. "What does that mean?"

"Glad you asked." Uncle Will beamed at T.J. "When sailors can't use the stars or points on land to steer by, then they must rely on compass alone. Called dead reckoning. Of course, before they had modern instruments, it was worse."

"Where's the kitten?" demanded Auntie Onion.

"Do you think I'd leave a man overboard?" asked Uncle Will indignantly. "I put him back in the drawer with the others, so's not to fret Flotsam.

But you can bet your brass buttons on this," he declared, shaking the fork. "That little explorer is not going to stay put for long."

"Explorer!" Now it was names, not numbers, that T.J. was ticking off on her fingers. DeSoto? No, one was enough. Columbus? Maybe . . . "Captain Cook!"

"A famous navigator," Uncle Will agreed. "Sailed the Pacific from New Zealand to Alaska . . ."

"A name for the kitten. Captain Cook!"

"Just perfect." Auntie Onion got up to clear the table. "I believe I'll call her Cookie for short."

Uncle Will grimaced. "Then *I'll* call him Cap."

They kept on squabbling, although neither of them knew whether Captain Cook was a boy or a girl. "Maybe it will answer to both nicknames," T.J. said tactfully. She picked up her plate. "Can we run the dishwasher tonight? I'd hate to get my new ring wet."

When she went up to her room at bedtime, T.J. found Flotsam and all four kittens, even Captain Cook, curled snugly in the dresser drawer. The black-and-white one had nestled beneath its mother's whiskers, so T.J. had to nudge it aside to scratch Sam under her chin.

T.J. dug the paper from her pocket before she exchanged her shirt and shorts for pajamas. She rolled down the long sleeves, for the evening was already damp, and leaned on the windowsill. Fog hung low on the horizon, as if waiting for some mysterious signal before creeping inland. The setting sun had smudged it with purple so that it looked like a bruise against the sky. Above the eucalyptus tree, a pale moon shone. It was lopsided and had a silvery ring around it. A moonbow, T.J. decided.

She lowered the window. Tomorrow, for sure, she'd give her ring to Walter. She wanted to hand it to him herself, to see how pleased he'd be. But even if he didn't come, if the foghorn didn't call, she could leave it on the old log. Either way, Walter would have a ring, and that would be almost as good as if he'd found his own. Thanks to her, he wouldn't have to hang around here for another hundred years.

T.J. took off the ring and put it on the dresser beside the zebra shell. The gold didn't seem as shiny as it had before, but even in the twilight the shell still glowed.

She turned on the lamp. It wasn't much brighter than a flashlight. Uncle Will was sure stingy about electricity, but she didn't have a lot left to read anyhow. T.J. yawned and unfolded the paper.

When the two men and the cabin boy reached land, they discovered a woman's body floating in the surf. They dragged her ashore, removed her earrings, and took a gold wedding band from her finger. Then they buried her in the sand, above the tidemark. The three made their way to a farmhouse, changed into dry clothes, borrowed a team of horses and continued their journey to San Francisco.

There wasn't any more, at least not about the *Coya*. T.J. frowned and held the paper beneath the light. Perhaps she was mistaken. But that was exactly what it said. " 'They dragged her ashore, removed her earrings, and took a gold wedding band from her finger,' " she read out loud.

His lost ring wasn't his at all. That Walter had looted from a dead body. Maybe he'd worn that poor lady's earrings, too, like the pirate he was. He was more than that. T.J.'s throat tightened. Someone who robbed the dead was a ghoul. The ghost boy was a body snatcher!

To think she'd felt sorry for a monster like that! Well, at least she'd found out in time. Now that she knew he didn't deserve that ring, ever, she certainly wasn't going to give him hers. T.J. got up and shoved the ring back on her finger. Then she crumpled up the newspaper and turned out the light.

Some noise awakened her, calling her out of her sleep. T.J. held her breath, listening.

She could hear the sound of the ocean, wave after wave pounding against the rocks. It sounded so close that for a moment she thought she was hearing her own pulse in her ears. Then something skittered on the roof overhead, and a bug, a big one, bumped against the windowpane. A branch on the Monterey pine scraped against the siding of the house and made her scalp tingle, like the scratch of a fingernail on a blackboard. Then the foghorn moaned, "Teee-Jay-a-ay!"

That was what she'd been dreading. She sat up abruptly. "No!" she answered. "Never again!"

Her own voice was comforting to hear. She looked around, but it was so dark, she could not even see the ceiling above her head. All she could make out was the outline of the window, a pale-gray rectangle floating in the darkness opposite her bed. She was sure she had shut it, but even so she could feel the chill of the fog, silent as smoke, drifting in around the frame.

If fog could slip through a closed window, so might a ghost. Walter might know she had a gold ring, and come for it. Unseen in the dark, he could reach out and snatch the ring from her finger. She clenched her hand into a fist.

Her mouth was dry. T.J. licked her lips. She wished she dared to get a drink of water, but the bathroom was at the end of the hall. Lying here in the dark was bad enough, but going down that creepy corridor would be worse.

Across the room a kitten squealed. Perhaps that ghoul would try to steal Sam again, even though he'd said he could not have a cat. Walter Cooper was a liar, too.

Although she was limp as seaweed, T.J. was determined to stay awake. She was going to keep her eyes wide open, all night, on guard. She would not even blink.

12

"Two bells and all's well!" called Uncle Will outside her door.

T.J. heard his feet clomp down the hall. He must be wearing his boots. Two bells. He'd explained ship's time, if she wasn't too sleepy to remember.

Midnight was eight bells. Then you had to begin counting over, adding a bell for each half hour. If 12:30 was one bell, two bells was 1:00 A.M. It was certainly later than that. That gray outside was daylight. You had to number the bells every four hours, so it would be another two bells at 5:00 A.M. But if it was that early, Uncle Will would still be shuffling around in his sheepskin slippers. Why the heck couldn't sailors wear watches like everyone else?

9:00 A.M. Two bells again. She'd really slept in! T.J. rubbed her eyes. Sandy. That reminded her of the beach, the ocean, and that reminded her of . . .

She should not have gone to sleep at all. T.J. rushed over to the dresser.

"One, two, three, four . . . five!" she counted and exhaled in relief. All was well with the cats, at least. But it might not go so well for her. If it was still gloomy so late in the morning, that meant it was foggy. And fog meant the foghorn. And the foghorn blowing meant *him*, coming back for the ring. Perhaps coming for her ring, too.

T.J. jerked it from her finger. Separating the tangle of kittens, she reached beneath them and thrust the ring into the pocket of her sweater. Flotsam purred loudly, as if to thank T.J. for this extra attention to her family. T.J. fluffed the kittens back into place, knotted her bathrobe, and hurried down to the kitchen before she might hear the foghorn.

Auntie Onion was flipping pancakes at the stove. "You must have been pretty tuckered out," she greeted T.J.

"I sure am," T.J. admitted.

"A few hotcakes will fix you up. Your uncle managed to pack away seven, but I held back some batter for you."

Auntie Onion put five pancakes, big as saucers, on T.J.'s plate. They were striped with yellow, like Captain Cook, and there was raspberry jam to go on top.

"Special breakfast. Is it another special day?" asked T.J. hopefully.

"Not that I know of," Auntie Onion replied.

"But we're going somewhere, aren't we?"

"We spent most all of yesterday at the Boardwalk," Auntie Onion pointed out.

"Let's do it again!" pleaded T.J.

Auntie Onion shook her head. "Can't run through life on repeats."

"It's foggy!" T.J. wailed. She couldn't stay here!

"So it is," said her aunt, glancing out the window. "Mother Nature's air conditioning. I suppose it might be sunny inland. We could go over to the redwood trees."

T.J. didn't care if the trees were orange or lavender, so long as they didn't grow anywhere near the beach. "I love the woods!" she said emphatically. "And we could take Winston, too."

"I don't think that's wise. Poor lad has a weak stomach. But there's always your Uncle Will. . . ."

"Great!" She would escape.

T.J. ran her finger along the edge of her plate to catch the last pink juice from the raspberry jam. Auntie Onion puckered her forehead, but said only, "You're not wearing your ring."

"It felt . . . a little tight," T.J. answered.

"Snug enough to leave its mark," agreed Auntie Onion.

T.J. looked down. There was a telltale green band where the ring had been. "My finger's turned green!"

"Cheap metal," said Auntie Onion.

"But the man said it was gold . . ."

"No, he didn't say that exactly. But he was glad to let you think it." Auntie Onion rinsed T.J.'s plate in the sink.

"A thing like that is just plain mean!" said T.J. indignantly.

"Yes." Her aunt raised her voice over the running water. "Things aren't always what they seem."

The redwood grove was called Big Basin. Giant trees stretched up so high that sunbeams were laced right into their topmost branches. Below, everything was in shadow, hushed. A carpet of pine needles muffled their footsteps and even Auntie Onion whispered. Everything in the woods seemed spellbound, but it was different from a spell of fog. Nothing unexpected could happen here. Or, if it did, it was good. A deer, a young buck with half-grown antlers, came so close that T.J. almost touched him.

There were noises, of course, but not the kind that raised goosebumps on her arms. Not like the foghorn. These were ordinary sounds. Birds called and squirrels scolded as they walked past. The jays were not so blue as Ohio jays, and the squirrels were gray, not red like those at home, but the sandwiches were peanut butter, without onions or sand.

T.J. delayed leaving as long as possible, asking

Uncle Will all kinds of questions and dragging behind whenever she could. When they were home at last, she locked her bedroom window, pulled down the shade, shut her door, and pushed a chair against it. No ghoulish ghost would sneak in tonight, not if she could help it.

At bedtime, Auntie Onion marched into T.J.'s room, knocking over the chair with a clatter.

"I got caught in a booby trap!" she exclaimed. She crossed the room and raised the shade. "It's dark as a grave in here." She opened the window. "And stuffy besides." Auntie Onion bent over the dresser drawer and sniffed. "Cats! Sure as hornets like honey, that sweater needs another wash."

"Not yet!" cried T.J. The ring was still in the pocket.

"Well, it's your funeral." Auntie Onion straightened up. "Leave your door open. Flotsam has to get in and out, you know."

"All right." T.J. didn't have much choice. She rapped her knuckles on the dresser top. Knock on wood that only Sam came in or out. She'd have to leave her door open, but sure as hornets like honey, she was going to bolt her window.

"Good night, sleep tight, don't let the cat fleas bite," said Auntie Onion.

13

Sun shone through the splits in the worn windowshade, turning each zigzag crack into a streak of lightning. When T.J. snapped up the blind, the brightness of the morning made her blink. Good weather, not ghost weather. Still . . .

"What's up?" asked T.J. as soon as she reached the kitchen, adding, "Besides me." For certain Auntie Onion had a plan for such a nice day.

"I thought I'd do the wash," her aunt replied. "And sun dry it."

"Why don't you hie yourself down to the beach?" asked Uncle Will.

"Not alone!" T.J. protested. Even if she wouldn't hear the foghorn, even if she never set eyes on that ghoulish boy again, she'd have the feeling he was out there somewhere, watching her.

Uncle Will looked at Auntie Onion and waggled his eyebrows. She puckered hers in return and said finally, "The elephant seals?"

"Elephant seals!" exclaimed T.J. right away. "Gosh, we don't have many of those in Cleveland."

"Doubtless not," agreed Uncle Will, "since this is the only place in the country they come ashore."

"If I don't see one now, I'll probably never get another chance in my whole life!"

Uncle Will grunted. "So go put on your safari togs."

Clean clothes of any sort were getting scarce in the carton. T.J. put on the shirt and shorts she'd worn yesterday. She would have gone in her pajamas if she had to. Auntie Onion and Uncle Will could program her like a computer for the rest of her stay, just so long as she never had to hear a foghorn calling "Tee-Jay-a-ay!"—calling the boy to "Come back!"

T.J. buckled herself in the backseat of the DeSoto, ready to be transported to faraway places. But the car had scarcely gotten up speed before Uncle Will turned off the road and pulled the key from the ignition.

"Disembark!" he ordered. "Año Nuevo State Park. Prepare to be astounded!"

T.J. followed her aunt and uncle past some

straggly trees and down a gravel road. The air was warm and smelled faintly of Brussels sprouts. Occasional wildflowers bloomed in the weedy brush that lined the road, and T.J. spied a gopher poking a toothy face from its hole. Interesting, but not exactly amazing. When the road ended, dunes took over. Small sand mountains rose and dipped before them, on and on.

"Año Nuevo means New Year in Spanish," Uncle Will said, panting up a hill. "Named by the explorer Viscaino on January 3, 1603. He did not land, of course."

Smart fellow, Viscaino. He didn't have to hike. T.J. stopped to empty sand from her shoes and then hurried to catch up to her aunt and uncle. The three trudged on in silence for another mile. When they finally crested the rise above the beach, a strange noise shook the stillness. T.J. stiffened. She had heard that noise before. It sounded like that ghost blowing on a kelp pipe. He couldn't be here!

T.J. turned to Auntie Onion and Uncle Will. Had they heard it, too, or was it just her ears? Then it sounded again, much louder and lower, like that funny rumble some plumbing makes if air's caught in the pipes when the water's turned on.

Uncle Will patted her head and pointed. "Look there!"

T.J. looked. Something was there, all right. Something the size of beached whales lay at the water's edge. They had ugly snouts that reminded her of those rubber bulbs you squeezed to blow a horn. One was wheezing right now and making that terrible noise. "Sea monsters!" T.J. gasped.

"There aren't any such things," said Uncle Will, "although long ago sailors believed these were monsters. They're genuine elephant seals!"

"Wow!" said T.J., because she couldn't think of anything else to say. These had to be ten times bigger than any seals she'd seen at a zoo.

"Elephant seals come ashore in the summer to molt old skin. Some older bulls, a lot of younger bachelors."

Bachelors figured. Who'd want a mate with a face like that? "What happened to their noses?" T.J. asked.

"That's how they earned their name. A male grows a snout like an elephant's trunk and can bellow like one, too."

"So I heard," T.J. answered, holding her own nose. The elephant seals didn't smell any better than they looked. She sat down on the dune, shoulder to shoulder with Auntie Onion, to watch them. Patches of fuzzy sealskin were scattered about the beach, blowing in the wind like scraps of Velcro. But the splotchy-backed elephant seals themselves were no busier than hunks of driftwood. T.J. waited five minutes before one even lifted a flipper to scatter sand on his back.

"Winter's when the action is," said Uncle Will.

"Thousands of elephant seals on the beach then. Bulls and cows, pups and weaners."

"Pups and weiners!" T.J. giggled. "Hot dogs!"

"Better not try spreading mustard on any of those bulls," her uncle warned. "If one should roll over on you, *SPLAT!*" Uncle Will stomped his boot. "Now, this kind of weaner is one who no longer needs mother's milk . . ."

T.J. was barely listening. The ocean was smooth and shiny, unrolling before them like a sheet of aluminum foil. It looked as if it stretched all the way to . . . No, not Australia. China. Just a bit offshore was a tiny island with a forlorn-looking building on it. Five chimneys stuck up from a broken-down roof, and the windows, missing their glass, stared back at her.

"What's that?" she asked, pointing.

"The lighthouse keeper's place."

"It looks spooky," said T.J. "Where's the lighthouse?"

"Fell down," Uncle Will replied. "It was old, although not so old as Pigeon Point."

T.J. kept on staring at the island. The perfect place for a shipwrecked haunt to hide would be a deserted house. She caught her breath. There was a shadow at one of the windows. "Something's in there!" she cried.

"Lots of somethings." Uncle Will chuckled. "Sea lions make themselves right at home."

"But no . . . people?"

"Been abandoned for more'n forty years. Light-house keeper drowned, too. Went down in his boat with his family. Why, the ghost stories I could tell you about these parts!"

"William!" Auntie Onion said sharply. She had taken off her shoe to inspect her heel, but now she glared at Uncle Will.

"But I think I'll tell you about seals and sea lions instead," Uncle Will said quickly. "Watch the way they go under water and you'll see the difference. Sea lions dive, seals just sink. Both have flippered feet, so both are pinnipeds . . ."

Auntie Onion unplugged her hearing aid.

August 19 A.M.   Pinniped   Flippered feet

She had been ignoring her word list, but this one was too good to skip. Not that Jana would go for a word like pinniped, but she bet her sixth-grade teacher would flip over it.

T.J. put down her notepad and went over to close the window. The night was nice, and a billion stars were out. Just five more nights to go and she'd be home. Then she could forget about ghosts and rings and foghorns. It would all seem like a bad dream, or like something you'd had once but had gotten over, like the chicken pox.

Kittens were scrabbling about in the drawer. A nice, friendly sound. Elephant seals were astounding, all right, but cats made better roommates. She

108

gave a pat to each one, climbed into bed, and pulled the cover up to her chin.

During the night, the blanket slid off and clammy fog poured in the window. In the morning, T.J.'s bed felt like the freezer bin in a supermarket and her toes were like Popsicles.

T.J. went down to the kitchen to thaw out. The air was foggy here, too, but that was because Auntie Onion had her right foot soaking in a pan of steaming water. From time to time she added more from the whistling teakettle.

"Yesterday I walked a blister on my heel the size of a sand dollar," she complained.

"I'm sorry," said T.J., and she was, but mostly for herself. She could beg or blubber, but there wouldn't be any outing today.

When Uncle Will came down for breakfast, he was cranky, too. In answer to T.J.'s "Good morning," he grumbled, "That tiger stripe was out of the drawer again. Wrenched my back hauling him from under your bed. And there was a wet spot on your rug."

"I'm sorry," said T.J. again, although she didn't see why it should be her fault.

"Time to move those kittens back downstairs," Auntie Onion decided. "Into a box in the kitchen, with newspapers."

"The cats keep me company at night," T.J. objected.

Uncle Will poured himself some coffee. "If you're

asleep, you don't need company." He took a sip, and his pink face turned red. He'd burned his tongue.

There wasn't any point in arguing. "I'll fix it," said T.J., and went back upstairs.

She dumped her clothes from the carton, took it to the kitchen, and lined it with newspaper. Then she carried the squirming kittens down and tucked them in. They did not seem to mind, and Flotsam was not around to disapprove. Next T.J. gathered up all her clothes and put them in the washing machine. She measured the soap and turned the dial to lukewarm, so nothing would shrink. It was too late to save her sweater, but before she tossed it in the washer, she fished her ring from the pocket. It was dull. She slipped the ring on her finger anyway, for safekeeping.

T.J. sat down at the table to catch her breath. Her aunt peered at her over her glasses and asked, "Did you put in enough soap?"

"I do the wash at home sometimes," T.J. said in answer.

Then her uncle asked, "Where's the sports page?"

T.J. gulped. "Is that the green sheet?"

Uncle Will nodded.

"I think . . . the newspaper's in the kitten carton."

Uncle Will opened his mouth, but he must have thought better of whatever he was going to say. He went over to the box and pushed the kittens aside. "This black and white one's stuck to my paper like a barnacle!"

"Hey!" T.J. exclaimed. "Let's call it Barnacle Bill!"

"All right," Auntie Onion agreed, but without enthusiasm. She poured more hot water.

"The Giants lost!" groaned Uncle Will. His voice rose up from the box like a moan from a cavern.

A bad beginning for a bad day. T.J. wandered into the living room and looked over the bookshelf. There wasn't a single mystery, and most of the volumes didn't even have pictures. She did find a small gray book with a gold lighthouse etched on the cover. *Captain January.* The flyleaf said, "To Elizabeth on her eleventh birthday." The book smelled like moldy bread.

T.J. turned the pages. There was a girl named Starbright and a crusty old lighthouse keeper. He was Captain January. She read some more. It was sort of interesting, but there wasn't enough talking. At least the book that she and Jana were writing had plenty of conversation. T.J. got up, put the clothes in the dryer, and came back to the living room, avoiding any talking of her own with Auntie Onion and Uncle Will.

She was on page twenty-three when the foghorn called.

T.J. froze. For the past three days, whenever a train whistled or a gull shrieked, she'd thought

111

she'd heard the foghorn. Out of the corner of her eye, she'd think she saw that ghost-ghoul. Her own reflection, caught in a window at dusk, made her jump.

Now that she'd really heard the foghorn, she'd really see him, too. Funny, but she didn't feel panicky. She was almost glad. Once she'd faced Walter with the truth, neither he nor the foghorn could ever haunt her again.

She got her jeans and sweatshirt from the dryer, both still a little damp, and put them on. "I'm going out," she said to her aunt and uncle. "I want to walk on the beach while the tide's low."

As she closed the back door, she almost tripped over Flotsam, curled up like a doorstop on the welcome mat. Flotsam looked reproachfully at T.J., then stretched her legs as if to get up and come along.

"Go in and look after your family, Sam," said T.J. "This time I'd better go alone."

T.J. turned and ran down the path to the beach before she could change her mind.

14

Walter did not see her. He had a stick and was poking about the smaller rocks, exposed at low tide, scraping away the moss. He didn't look as frightening as T.J. had expected. As before, he was drenched with saltwater. Her own sweatshirt wasn't exactly warm and dry either, but she intended to get everything over with as quickly as she could. Still, she hesitated and hung back by the old log. She didn't know whether she was afraid of asking Walter the questions or of the answers he might give her.

"Tee-Jay-a-ay!" the foghorn called softly.

It was scarcely louder than a whisper, but at once the boy straightened and turned. "Miss Theresa! I thought I'd not set eyes on you again."

113

"I wish I'd never seen you to begin with, Walter Cooper," T.J. blurted.

The boy dropped the stick. "What did I do to rile you now?" he asked. Then his why-pick-on-me tone of voice changed. "I will thank you not to call me Walter Cooper. That's not my name, nor one I care to hear."

"It was in the paper, so it's true," said T.J. "Walter was—you were—the *Coya*'s cabin boy."

"That's the truth, far as it goes." He picked up the stick and began to dig in the sand around the rocks. "A lazy bloke, that Walter. He jolly well had the title of cabin boy, but 'twas me did all his chores."

"You mean . . . you're not Walter?"

"That's what I told you," the boy answered.

"But the paper would have said if there were two boys," T.J. persisted.

"Those signed on, right enough. But I came on the ship unannounced, so to speak. I was what some call a skip-and-stray."

Did they have to go around on this again? T.J. sighed and tapped a finger against her forehead.

"A stowaway." He grinned at her. "When Captain Paige found me hiding in the hold, he could have thrown me into the moan-and-wail—that's jail—but he allowed I might work for my passage."

"An honest-to-gosh stowaway!" cried T.J., and then wished she hadn't. She wasn't going to let herself get taken in again. She'd only been here five minutes while he'd had more than a century to make up a good story. But when it came to being a detective, she'd had some practice herself. "Just answer true or false," she said. "You're looking for a gold wedding ring. True?"

"True."

"And Walter Cooper"—and maybe he's you, she thought—"he found one on a dead lady's hand and stole it."

"True."

"So," T.J. fumbled, "that ring that you want so much, it's not yours at all."

"False."

"But . . ."

"Give me a minute." He held up his hand to stop her. "The ring you read about did belong to Missus Jefferis. Walter had had his eye on it all along, so when she was quite plainly drowned, rest her soul, he helped himself."

"Ghoul!" muttered T.J., but she didn't look at the ghost boy as she said it.

"Not to be too hard on Walter, Miss," he said. "Gold makes the best of us greedy, and trinkets are of more use to the living than to the dead. Such things were done often then."

Maybe then. Not now. And who was he, anyway, to preach at her? T.J. scowled. "If that's so, why do you want a gold ring?"

"Ah, that's a different tale entirely, if you're willing to listen."

"I'm listening," said T.J. It had better be good.

"My ring was my English grandmother's, made for her by my English grandfather. He hammered it out hisself from a gold sovereign."

T.J. wrinkled her nose in disbelief.

"A sovereign's an English coin," he explained, mistaking her expression. "When my granny passed on, that ring came to my father to marry a wife of his own."

T.J. shrugged and watched a brown pelican flying overhead.

"My father had the ring in his pocket when he came Down Under. He dreamed of striking it rich in the gold rush."

"The gold rush!" T.J. looked him straight in the eye. Now she'd really caught this tale-telling ghost! "The gold rush was in America. In 1849, and right here in California."

"Have you not heard of the one in Australia? It began two years later, and it was there my father went. He found no gold dust, but a bride instead to wear his golden ring. She was my mother, quite bonny and red-haired like myself."

He waited expectantly, but T.J. wasn't going to give him the satisfaction of a single word.

"When I was thirteen, both of them died of the spotted fever," he said, swiping at his nose with the back of his hand. "And here I am."

"Last I knew you were in Australia."

"Who's to look out for an orphan? I hid away

116

on the *Coya* to get myself to San Francisco and seek a fortune of my own."

"I thought this story was about *your* gold ring," T.J. said.

"And so it is. 'Guard this ring with your life' were the last words my mother spoke. So I promised her I'd keep it with me always. I'd not give it, nor sell it, nor lose it."

"But you did!" T.J. exclaimed. "You lost the ring right here!"

"Aye, and lost my life, too, and don't you forget it, Miss!" he shouted in her ear. "The both of them washed away by a wave."

T.J. stood her ground. He couldn't prove who he was, so he couldn't prove what he said was true, either. "How do I know you're not really Walter Cooper?"

"Because that sea dog had the good fortune not to drown."

For Pete's sake! Why hadn't she thought of that? Walter had changed into dry clothes when he got to land! This ghost boy was soaking wet. "I guess I've been mistaken," she admitted.

The ghost boy gave her a sly look. "Mistaken identity, you might say."

"One gold ring is like another," said T.J., pulling the ring from her finger. "Take this. You can rub off the 'Santa Cruz' with sand."

"Uncommon kind of you," he answered, gently

waving it away. "But 'twouldn't do for me at all."

T.J. slipped the ring back onto her finger and jammed her hands into her pockets. Of course her ring would not be right. She should have figured that out, too. "Do you think your ring—your mother's—could still be here?"

"Things long buried in the sea bed may surface sudden with the tide. I have reckoned to search in this place because this is where the horn calls loudest."

"For me, too," said T.J.

She suddenly bent over and took off her shoes. Then she rolled her jeans up to her knees and shoved the sleeves of her sweatshirt above her elbows.

"Maybe you've got forever," T.J. declared. "But I've only got four more days around here." She began digging damp sand from a crevice. "So let's get cooking!"

The ghost boy looked puzzled for a moment and then, "Looking!" he shouted.

He dropped to his hands and knees beside her. The two of them searched in silence until the tide came in and the sun came out.

15

T.J. caught a whiff of frying bacon, but something far more important than breakfast was on her mind. It had occurred to her as soon as she got up, even before she'd washed her face. If Walter wasn't the ghost boy's name, then what was it? She'd never even asked him. She grabbed Winston's crumpled newspaper from the dresser top.

"Nuts!"

Her memory hadn't been playing tricks. It was just what she'd read before. The paper did not mention an extra boy aboard the *Coya*.

> It was rumored that among the losses was a thirteen-year-old stov—

Stove? That might be the word lost in the crease. Or it might be the bacon talking, making *stove* pop into her head. It could be a completely different word. T.J. couldn't think of any other, and she'd put the dictionary back in the bookshelf, downstairs. She stared at the paper, turning it sideways and upside down. If that *v* was really part of a *w*, then . . .

"Stowaway!" she yelped. The ghost boy hadn't been fibbing to her. He had not been overlooked after all. But she still did not know his name.

Working the word out had been easy. The hard work came an hour later, after breakfast, when T.J. tried to persuade her great-aunt to let her go down to the shore.

"Jumping junipers!" declared Auntie Onion. "You're more changeable than the weather. You blow hot about the ocean one day, cold the next. I thought we'd make some cookies . . ."

"It's too nice to stay in today," begged T.J. Too terribly nice. With this sunshine, she wasn't likely to see so much as the boy's shadow, even if he could cast one. She'd have to look for the ring alone. "Maybe Winston's at the beach," she persisted. "I've got this paper to give back to him."

"Well . . ."

T.J. sighed loudly. "I suppose if I can't go there, I can't go anywhere. Because of your blister."

"Dratted nuisance!" Auntie Onion looked down and scowled. A tennis shoe was laced on her left foot, but she wore Uncle Will's comfy sheepskin slipper on her right. "Suit yourself," she said at last.

The ghost boy wasn't there. Neither was Winston, although he'd been around earlier, for there was a giant *WDO* scratched in the sand. T.J. rubbed it out and began her hunt. She dug in the most sheltered spots, shifting rocks and heavy ropes of kelp. After two hours her arms were sore and all the sand began to look the same. The sun was too hot. She either froze or roasted at the seashore, no in-betweens. The tide had started to come in, each wave frothing higher on the shore before it slid back into the sea. She might as well quit. Hunting might be better tomorrow, and she had three days left to look for the ring.

"Not again!" T.J. exclaimed the next morning. She could not believe that Auntie Onion and Uncle Will had planned another excursion without her even asking.

"I know just the thing to pull you out of your doldrums," Uncle Will assured her.

"I don't want to be pulled anywhere!" T.J. wailed. "I want to hang around here." The weather was exactly right, overcast, and the tide was out.

"Pescadero's our port today," Uncle Will said firmly.

"Mostly we'll just joyride," added Auntie Onion, holding her slippered foot aloft.

121

"Anchors aweigh!" Uncle Will called over his shoulder as he headed out to the car.

T.J. sulked in the backseat of the car. She was mad enough to spit toads, but mostly angry at herself. If she hadn't pestered to go places before, they wouldn't be dragging her along now. Every mile or so she groaned, but Auntie Onion couldn't hear and it only made Uncle Will twice as cheerful.

"Pescadero's a Portuguese fishing village," he said. "Quaint!"

As far as T.J. was concerned, the quaintest thing about the whole trip was the thistle soup they had for lunch. The restaurant made it from artichokes. By the time they returned, it was high tide. All she had to show for the day was another word for her list.

August 20 A.M.   doldrums   A place in the ocean where ships got stuck. Me too.

If she didn't find the ring tomorrow, or the day after, both she and the ghost boy were sunk.

D for disaster. That was how the following day began. The first bad sign was the summer sun blazing overhead. The second thing to go wrong was Uncle Will. He started to tag along to the beach.

"So you won't be alone."

No way T.J. could discourage him without being

rude, so she was. "I don't want you to come. It's an adventure if I go by myself."

Uncle Will looked hurt. He turned on his heel and headed for home without saying a word.

T.J. felt guilty. How could she explain that everything was different now? He'd think she was wombatty if she told him she was searching for a ring lost by a drowned stowaway over one hundred and twenty years ago.

It was easier to talk to Winston. She could hardly avoid him because he was already there.

"I'm treasure hunting," said T.J. "Want to help?"

"Sure," Winston agreed. "What are we looking for?"

"Anything. Everything," T.J. answered.

"Sometimes you find Indian arrowheads, but this beach isn't the best one."

"It's good enough for me," said T.J.

Winston was a super sleuth when it came to beachcombing. He marked the sand out in a grid, like a colossal tic-tac-toe game. Each of them thoroughly searched a square before going on to another. Hunting like this was rewarding. Winston found a piece of rose-colored glass, which he gave to T.J., a cork from a fishing net, and an almost perfect crab shell, which he kept. Then T.J. dug up a fragment from something glossy and white, with yellow lines scrolled along the edge.

"Scrimshaw!" Winston determined. "Whale-bone, I bet."

Uncle Will would love whalebone. It would make up for not bringing him along. When T.J. tucked it into her pocket, she remembered the paper. It was still in her jeans, and she'd changed into shorts because long pants were too warm.

"I forgot to bring your newspaper," she apologized.

"Who needs it?" asked Winston. "I'm writing about something much better now. Sea monsters!"

"There aren't any such animals," T.J. said scornfully.

"So?" Winston smirked. "I even know what a sea monster eats for dinner."

"What?"

"Fish and ships!"

T.J. did not think that was very funny. And they did not find anything else that morning worth mentioning.

16

"Washed out!" muttered T.J., turning from the tide table. The next low water wasn't until 6:00 P.M., smack in the middle of supper. She sniffed. Something was in the oven now. "Smells good!" she said loudly.

"I finally stirred up those Oatmeal Jumbles," Auntie Onion replied. "They're a bit scorched on the bottom, but I scraped them. I ran out of oatmeal, so I filled in with Rice Krispies, and I didn't have any nuts so I used . . ."

"Onions?"

"Of course not!" Auntie Onion threw up her hands as if she'd never heard of such a thing. "Raisins."

"I'll take a cookie up to Uncle Will," said T.J.,

125

helping herself to three. "I've got something to show him."

Uncle Will didn't even look up when she climbed into the Crow's Nest. T.J. had to clear her throat before he turned and said gruffly, "I'm busy." Then he spotted the cookies. "For me?"

"They're still warm." T.J. handed him one.

Uncle Will chewed without talking. Obviously he was still annoyed with her. "How come it's called a crow's nest?" T.J. ventured at last. "On a ship it should be a gull's nest."

Uncle Will had another cookie. "Ancient sailors always took a crow to sea in case they lost their bearings. Then they'd release the bird from its perch on top of the mast. A crow flies to the nearest land, so they would sail in that direction."

"Is that true?"

"Maybe. Maybe not." Uncle Will fell silent.

T.J. tried again. "I brought you something else." She handed him the decorated fragment she'd found on the beach.

Uncle Will held it up to the sunlight shining through the porthole window and squinted. "Why would I want a piece of trash?" he asked peevishly.

"Winston said it was scrimshaw. Whalebone."

"It's plastic!" Uncle Will snorted. "A piece broken from one of those can't-bust-'em dinnerplates. Now I'll show you what *real* scrimshaw looks like . . ."

He went over to the curio cabinet, turned the

key, and swung open the glass door. T.J. held her nose. Dead seashells.

"There!" Uncle Will pointed to the shark's tooth. A tiny clipper ship in full sail was etched on one side. "Sailors used to carve scrimshaw to while away long hours at sea," he began.

T.J. let go of her nose and peered into the cabinet. Toward the back of the second shelf, in a heap of buttons, was a thin circle of gold. "That ring! Where did it come from?"

"Found it here on our beach, years ago." He picked up the ring. "Homemade, from the looks of it. Probably some poor sailor's wedding band."

T.J. got so excited that she crumbled the last cookie. "Uncle Will, can I have it?"

"Certainly not. You've got a ring already."

"But this one isn't right . . . and I think that one is!"

"You're making crumbs."

T.J. wiped her fingers. Her palms were getting sweaty. "I've got to have it, Uncle Will!"

"Someday a nice young fellow will give you a wedding ring of your own."

"Please!" T.J. was practically crying. The ring had been here all along, waiting for her. She couldn't just let it sit there in a pile of—of junk! "I'll trade you! You can have my zebra."

"The Amoria? The zebra volute?"

"A shell will look better in your case. More oceany than an old ring."

127

"Nautical," Uncle Will corrected. He pursed his lips and looked up at the ceiling. "Perhaps if you find something else . . ."

"Anything!" promised T.J.

"Not garbage like that plastic, and give me both . . ."

"Shame on you!"

T.J. and Uncle Will jumped. Two hands, white knuckled, gripped the iron railing, and Auntie Onion's gray head and shoulders appeared in the opening to the Crow's Nest.

"What in tarnation do you think you're doing, Elizabeth?" shouted Uncle Will.

"I'm sticking my nose in your business," said Auntie Onion, "but that's all of me that's coming up here. I was down below, where it's good and solid, and could hear you talking. But I couldn't quite make out what . . ."

"Eavesdropper!" mumbled Uncle Will, but she didn't hear that, either.

"I never intended to scale your ladder, just put a foot on it and listen. When I heard you being stubborn as always . . ."

"Me!"

". . . Stubborn and selfish," Auntie Onion continued. "T.J. offered to trade you fair and square for that ring. She was tricked by one flimflam clown at the Boardwalk and I won't have her bamboozled by another."

"Invading a man's privacy just to stir up a fuss!"

sputtered Uncle Will. He glared at Auntie Onion, wiped his forehead with his pocket hankerchief, hesitated, and then dropped the ring into T.J.'s hand. "I was going to swap with you anyway." He stamped back to his desk and said loudly, "Name-calling is very childish."

"I'm making a new batch of cookies with those butterscotch chips you love, Will," answered Auntie Onion. "Found some hiding in a coffee can."

Auntie Onion's head disappeared and T.J. could hear the slap of her slipper and the thud of her shoe as she backed down the iron rungs, one by one. From the bottom her aunt called, "If you want any cookies, you'll have to come down and get them yourself. I'll not climb this contraption again!"

Uncle Will looked over his shoulder and waggled his eyebrows at T.J.

"Thanks a million, Uncle William," she said.

T.J. was practically one hundred percent certain it was the ghost boy's ring. She could see the markings of a coin beneath the tiny hammer dents. Her Boardwalk ring had been brighter when it was new, but this one had the kind of gleam that wouldn't rub off. She wrapped it in a piece of tissue and put it on her dresser. First thing in the morning, she'd give the long-lost ring back to the stowaway.

T.J. was restless. Her heart was going too fast and the clock seemed to be going too slow. She wandered into the living room.

Captain January was over the arm of the couch, just where she'd left it three days ago. T.J. picked it up. The lighthouse in the book was called Storm Castle. It was tall and white, like the lighthouse at Pigeon Point.

" 'A gray day! soft gray sky, like the breast of a dove, sheeny gray sea . . .' " T.J. read aloud.

Soft gray sky. If it were like that tomorrow, she would be sure to see the ghost boy. And hear the foghorn. Nothing was said about a foghorn in the book. Maybe the author was absentminded.

T.J. thumbed through the pages, but she couldn't concentrate. Talk about absentminded! Her mind just wouldn't connect, or perhaps it was connecting too well. Her thoughts were linked together like the paper chains she'd made in kindergarten.

She could understand why the foghorn wanted the ghost boy to come back here, because this is where his ring was. But why right now? Uncle Will would never lose it. If it weren't for her, that ring would still be locked up tight in his curio cabinet.

T.J. flipped to the end of the book. " 'For Captain January's last voyage is over and he is already in the haven where he would be.' "

She read it aloud as *heaven* first because that seemed to fit the sentence. When she realized the word was different, she crossed the room and pulled the dictionary from the shelf. There it was, after *have* and before *have-not*. *Haven*: A sheltered harbor. A safe place.

The ghost boy's last voyage was over, too. But he couldn't go on to any haven without his ring. Or without her help. She was the only one who could return the ring. She was the link between the ghost and Uncle Will, and that was why the foghorn called her name. What if she hadn't listened?

T.J. closed the dictionary. "Please let it be a foggy morning," she whispered.

17

"Too bad it's overcast this morning," said Auntie Onion, "especially since it's your last full day with us."

"I like the fog," T.J. declared.

"You're whistling a different tune of late," her aunt commented. "I suppose you mean to scavenge the beach again."

T.J. nodded.

" 'All the day they hunted, and nothing did they find, But a ship a-sailing, a-sailing with the wind,' " quoted Uncle Will.

He knew a poem for everything. This one did not quite fit, for T.J. planned to *give* today, not get. "I won't be gone long," she promised.

"You'd better not be." Auntie Onion glanced at

the tide chart. "Water will be in by half past eleven."

"T.J.'s already learned that lesson," said Uncle Will. He eyed her rings. "As for meeting anyone on the beach, she's got a brass knuckle on each hand."

She wore both rings. The imitation gold was on her left hand, the real one on the middle finger of the right. That ring was much too loose and slid over her knuckle. T.J. smiled at her uncle. He was joking. She'd been afraid he might still be cross, or that he would insist on going with her. Uncle Will's jolliness came and went like the tides, and T.J. hadn't figured out his timetable.

T.J. whistled through her teeth as she wound her way down to the beach. She really had changed her tune about the fog. She liked the way the overcast put a silvery shine on everything, making even ordinary bushes look mysterious. Trees floated without roots and lost their tops in the soft gray mist.

She liked the way the fog smelled, sharp and prickly in her nostrils, like the first sniff of vinegar from a newly opened jar of pickles.

She liked the feel of the fog, cool on her cheeks. She had sunburned yesterday, but perhaps that would turn to tan by the time she was back in Cleveland.

Most of all, she liked the fog because it meant she would see him again. If only it were thicker, the pea soup kind, not so thin and patchy.

He was not perched on the flat-topped rock. That

was a letdown. She didn't want to leave the ring. She wanted to put it right into his hand. T.J. sat on the rock herself for a while, until she couldn't stand being still for another minute.

The tide had begun to drift in, but some of the smaller stones were not yet covered. T.J. hunted among them for hermit crabs. What appeared to be an empty snail case would suddenly sprout legs and scuttle away. Someone had lost a thong sandal, and it bobbed on top of the water like a miniature raft. Then, farther out, resting on the sandy bottom, T.J. spied a huge shell. She took off her socks and shoes, left them by the driftwood log, and waded cautiously into the surf.

She could see it better now. It was an abalone shell, pinkish red along the edge and mother-of-pearl inside. The closer she got, the larger the shell looked. It might even be bigger than the one in Uncle Will's cabinet, although that was hard to tell for sure because the water magnified everything. It was farther out than she had guessed. Water made distances difficult to judge, too. She rolled up her jeans and took one step at a time, holding on to a rock whenever a swell rolled in. She was bending down to grab the shell when the foghorn blew.

"TEE-JAY-A-AY!"

Was he here? The foghorn had never called her so insistently before. T.J. whirled around. She was

134

looking toward the beach when the wave hit. It struck her behind the knees, knocking her down as if she'd been tackled. The undertow pulled at her ankles. She couldn't get a foothold on the shifting sandy bottom, and the waves tumbled her over and over as if she were in a washing machine. As the water swirled over her head, she recalled Uncle Will's warning: "Never turn your back on the ocean."

Her nose was running, tickling like a carbonated drink coming up instead of going down. She must have swallowed a gallon of water, but she was thirsty and her throat scratched. Her tongue felt too big for her mouth, swollen and clumsy. T.J. opened her eyes. All she saw was sand. Her head was upside down and she was draped over the log like clothes spread out to air. How had she gotten here? T.J. could not remember.

"What are you doing?"

She wasn't doing anything. She couldn't. T.J. rolled over. Winston was standing above her. He'd been swimming. No, he wasn't wet. It was her eyes that were watery. She wiped them.

"You look awful lying there. Are you trying to dry out?"

T.J. sat up. "I—guess so." Her voice cracked, full of static like an old radio.

"I came to say good-bye," said Winston.

"You mean hello." He was as mixed up as she was. "You just got here."

"I've been hanging around waiting for you to wake up."

"Why good-bye?" asked T.J. Perhaps he thought she was dying.

"Because you're going back to Ohio tomorrow, aren't you?"

"Maybe." T.J. didn't know whether it was today, tomorrow, or yesterday. You can't tell time in a dream.

"So," said Winston, "so long." He held out his hand.

Her arm weighed a ton. Her sweatshirt clung to it, limp and heavy. It was hard to lift it up, but she managed to shake Winston's hand. Something was wrong.

The ghost boy's ring was missing! She wasn't wearing it. The other was still on her left hand, but on the right—the one Winston kept pumping— the middle finger was bare.

Winston *had* thought she was dead! When he'd seen her lying on the beach, he'd pulled off the gold band. He'd looted, just as Walter Cooper had from that drowned lady. She glared at him. "You took my ring!"

Winston dropped her hand like he'd been stung by a jellyfish. "Winston Osborn does not steal!" he yelled. "And if he did, I'd take your abalone shell."

T.J. looked down. Beside the log was the abalone shell, even bigger than she'd imagined. But she didn't care about that. "My ring is gone," she moaned.

"Well, don't expect me to help you look for it."

"Why . . . not?" asked T.J. groggily.

"Because you called me a thief, that's why." Winston, barefoot, stamped down the beach.

His feelings were hurt. T.J. could tell by the way he hunched his shoulders, but she did not call him back. She sat on the log, holding her head. She still felt fuzzy. Maybe she'd been unconscious. The last thing she could picture in her mind was reaching for that shell. It seemed so long ago, but it couldn't have been. Although the sun was shining now, the tide had not moved in very far.

The ring had been on her finger before she was knocked over by that wave. She must have lost it then, in the ocean, just as the stowaway had. Only she wasn't a ghost. She was alive.

It wouldn't hurt to look around on the beach anyway. But it did. Even standing up hurt, inside and out, as if she'd fallen off a horse instead of into an ocean. T.J. shaded her eyes and studied the sand. From the water's edge to the log was a long double track, like something had been dragged up the beach. Someone. Her. At the base of the flat rock several large words were written in the sand. Painfully, clothes sticking to her, T.J. picked her way over to them.

TRICKS AND PRANKS

Beside the three words was the sliver of green china that the writer must have used to scratch his message. T.J. put it in her pocket. She was a robot; everything was automatic.

Tricks and pranks. Winston wrote that. It was his idea of a joke, like fish and ships.

He must have pulled her from the water. Tough job for a little kid, and she had not even said thanks. Worse, she'd accused him of stealing.

T.J. put on her socks and shoes and picked up the abalone shell. She dreaded going back to the house. She could imagine what Auntie Onion would say when she saw her wet clothes, how disappointed Uncle Will would be that she'd lost the ring. She supposed she ought to be grateful she wasn't dead, grateful to be getting on a plane and flying home to Cleveland tomorrow.

Safe and sound.

18

"See what the cat dragged in!" exclaimed Auntie Onion as soon as T.J. appeared in the doorway.

She must have looked as bad as she felt. Sometimes Sam brought the remains of a gopher to the welcome mat. "I didn't mean to," T.J. began. Her voice trailed off as she tried to swallow the catch in her throat.

Auntie Onion gazed at her thoughtfully. "Of course you didn't," she said.

Uncle Will had scarcely noticed T.J. He directed his attention to the abalone shell. "You certainly meant to do that! A real beauty."

T.J. put it down on the table. She wished she could stop her hand from shaking. Uncle Will's eyes shifted from the shell to her fingers. "I lost the gold wedding ring," T.J. mumbled. "In the water." She leaned on the table and waited for him to snap "I told you so!" Or something worse.

Uncle Will patted her hand. Then he cleared his throat and murmured, "What came from the sea has gone back to the sea."

Perhaps it was what Uncle Will just said. Perhaps it was what he didn't say, or Auntie Onion either. Suddenly T.J. started to cry. These weren't quiet little sniffles but great noisy sobs. She hadn't bawled like this since she was seven, when she'd slammed her thumb in the car door. Once the tears began coming, T.J. couldn't stop them, any more than she could the tide.

"It's all right," Uncle Will repeated over and over. "You're all right."

Auntie Onion handed T.J. a whole roll of paper towels so that she could blow her nose. "What you need is a cup of cocoa," she said firmly.

T.J.'s teeth were chattering. Uncle Will made her sit down in a chair and wrapped the afghan around her shoulders. Auntie Onion poured some cocoa into one of her prettiest cups. T.J. felt a little better, except that the chocolate going down met sobs coming up and turned them into hiccups.

"Guess who's looking at you!" exclaimed Uncle Will. He held up the tiger stripe by the scruff of its neck. A round blue eye stared into T.J.'s puffy red ones. "Captain Cook is taking a peek at the world."

"He's . . ." T.J. gulped. "He's only got one eye!"

140

"The other will pop open soon. Maybe tomorrow."

T.J. gave the kitten a watery smile. "You look like a pirate."

"Ha!" chortled Uncle Will. "We should have named him Captain Hook!"

T.J. put the tiger back into the box. All the other kittens' eyes were still squeezed together, but there was something decidedly different about the calico.

"The calico's ears are standing up!" cried T.J. "They're not squashed flat to her head anymore."

"All the better for listening," explained Uncle Will. "A cat points its ears, like two antennas, to catch sounds."

"You mean . . . all this time . . ." T.J. sniffed, "I've been talking to the kittens and they couldn't really hear me?"

"Perhaps they did," comforted Auntie Onion. "I'm sure they recognized your voice."

T.J. hugged the calico. She scratched the orange spot under her chin, a mark identical to Flotsam's. If only Auntie Onion and Uncle Will would keep her, keep her right here by the ocean, where this special kind of calico cat belonged. They could call her Samantha. Of course, Uncle Will wouldn't think that was nautical enough, and Auntie Onion would get confused with two cats nicknamed Sam.

"Poor little kitten," T.J. whispered into the small triangle of an ear. "Not able to stay, no name at all, like the stowaway."

"I'm willing to bet that kitten pricked up her ears because she heard a foghorn, too," offered Uncle Will cheerfully.

"William!" warned Auntie Onion.

It was too late. T.J.'s eyes had started to puddle again.

Her nose was stuffy and her knees were still shaky when T.J. climbed the ladder to the Crow's Nest.

"Drop anchor," Uncle Will invited, pulling out the chair from his desk.

"I can't stay," said T.J. "I'm packing." She held out the zebra shell. "I came up to give you this."

"No, sir!" Uncle Will looked alarmed and pushed away her hand. "I won't take it."

"We made a bargain," T.J. insisted, "so it's yours."

"Bargain's off since you've not got the ring any longer."

"Fair's fair." T.J. stroked the zebra shell and then put it on the desk. "Maybe it's better in your cabinet than in my aquarium. Fresh water might fade it."

"Algae might make it a little fuzzy," Uncle Will allowed. He went over to the cabinet and unlocked the door. He put the zebra volute on the top shelf in front of the other shells. It looked right at home, even if it did come from the other side of the Pacific. "Are you sure?" he asked.

"I'm sure," said T.J. "I've got the abalone shell

anyway." Without question, hers was bigger than Uncle Will's. "I picked up something else today." She reached in her pocket. This time she placed a sliver of china on his desk.

Uncle Will was swinging the key, ready to return it to the drawer, when he saw the gleaming bit of green china. "Great Scott!" He threw up his hands and dropped the key. "Do you suppose? That looks as if . . . Where's that blasted key?"

T.J. helped him look. It seemed as if she'd spent most of this whole vacation on her hands and knees searching for something. When they finally found it, Uncle Will was panting. He opened the cabinet again with trembling fingers and lifted the chipped green plate from its rack. The sliver that T.J. had found lying beside the words in the sand fit perfectly. Even the red curlicues decorating the rim of the plate matched.

"A museum piece!" Uncle Will took a deep breath. "When it's properly mended, of course." He rubbed his hands. "China from China! Ming Dynasty. Must be at least four hundred years old."

"And it washed all the way over here?" asked T.J. doubtfully.

"No, no! Ships crossing the Pacific carried a few oriental treasures. The captains hoped to get fancy prices for them here in America." He shook his head. "But why you should find the missing piece now, that's the puzzle."

"It was just—there." She wouldn't lie, but she

143

wasn't going to do any more explaining than she had to. T.J. was certain her aunt and uncle already suspected how close she'd come to real trouble today.

"It's here now, that's the main thing." Uncle Will eased the plate back onto its holder and put the chip beside it. Then he reached for a book on his desk, flipped to the middle, and read aloud.

"God moves in a mysterious way,
   His wonders to perform;
He plants his footsteps in the sea,
   And rides upon the storm."

For the rest of the day, both her uncle and aunt treated T.J. as if she'd come down with some terrible sickness. They kept peeking into her room and checking on her. At supper, Uncle Will watched each bite she took, urging seconds and thirds on everything, and after supper Auntie Onion wouldn't even let her do the dishes.

"I didn't break an arm!" T.J. protested. "I can handle a dish towel."

Auntie Onion gave in and let T.J. dry, although every now and then she'd look up from the dishpan and sneak a worried glance at her. When they'd almost finished, Auntie Onion glanced at T.J.'s hand.

"You could try buffing that ring you got at the Boardwalk. A little toothpaste might take off the tarnish."

"Toothpaste!"

"Works on your teeth, doesn't it? When the ring's shiny, put on a coat of nail polish, and it won't turn your finger green."

"That's a neat idea," agreed T.J.

"I've got the paste, but I don't have the polish." Auntie Onion waved a hand, wrinkled from the dishwater. "No need for fancy fingers. Just keep them clean."

"I know who always has nail polish," T.J. said thoughtfully.

Of course, it was too late to borrow any from Winston now. She'd have to ask Jana for some when she got home. Probably Auntie Onion meant the clear kind anyway, and this morning Winston's toes were painted Halloween orange. T.J. could see him stamping away, heels digging holes in the sand and toes outshining the sun.

Why hadn't Winston left footprints when he dragged her up on the beach? He certainly should have, hauling a load like her. She weighed eighty-three pounds. She'd still been dazed, but she was certain she remembered correctly all the same. The picture of the parallel tracks her dangling legs had made in the sand was clear. There was no sign that anyone else had been there. Mysterious. Mysterious way. That was in the poem Uncle Will had read.

When the idea hit T.J., she almost dropped the teacup. There were no footprints in the sand because these had been footsteps from the sea!

"Careful!" her aunt exclaimed, catching the cup by the handle.

"Excuse me. I just thought of something, and I've got to write it down, quick!"

T.J. raced through the kitchen and up the stairs. She'd already packed her word list in the bottom of her suitcase. Flat things first. She dumped the contents of her bag on the floor and grabbed her pencil. Then she slowed down enough to print in careful letters.

August 23 A.M.   Tricks and Pranks   Thanks!!!

As hard as the stowaway had tried to teach her rhyming slang, she'd been awfully slow in catching on.

He was the one who had pulled her from the water. Of course he had been there. The foghorn had called, hadn't it, and who else could have gotten to her in time? He had written those words, and he had left the piece of china for Uncle Will, on purpose.

If the ghost boy had found her, then he must have found his ring as well. She'd done it! She *had* returned his ring.

T.J. went over to the window and tugged until she had it open wide. She stuck her head out and shouted into the twilight, "Thank *you*!"

She left the window open. It was a wonderful evening. No need for a foghorn tonight.

19

T.J. had to sit on her suitcase to close it. Things did not fit as well the second time around. At least she was leaving her sweater behind. The abalone shell took up a lot of room, and Auntie Onion had insisted that she pack *Captain January*. Perhaps she could sell it someday for a lot of money, since it was an honest-to-gosh antique. Or perhaps she'd keep it forever, because of the lighthouse on the cover.

This time she packed her word list on top where she could share it with Jana as soon as she got home. It was the start of a super secret code and better than anything she could have bought her. Besides, she was going to let Jana be the one to paste the sticker on Dave's car.

When T.J. hauled her suitcase down to the kitchen, she found Auntie Onion making sandwiches.

"I don't trust that doll-sized plastic tray that they give you for lunch on an airplane," she said.

T.J. would have to carry the sandwiches along with her. That was bound to be embarrassing. You could smell the onions right through the brown paper bag. One sniff and the attendant would put her way in the back row, by herself.

Uncle Will was pacing in circles around the kitchen table. Travel made him nervous. Anybody's. He was certain the plane would take off without him, even if he wasn't the one with the ticket.

"Stop growing worrywarts!" said Auntie Onion. "We've got two hours before we have to leave for the airport."

Uncle Will frowned, checked his watch, and then brightened. "There's time for a stroll on the beach." He whispered to T.J., "We might find something useful."

"Let's," she agreed.

The three of them had to march single file along the path through the weeds, but when they got to the dunes, Uncle Will took Auntie Onion's arm.

"A sore heel's enough. I can't have you turning an ankle."

T.J. sat down on the log and watched her great-aunt and uncle parade across the sand. They faced into the wind, and the breeze made Auntie Onion's dress balloon. Uncle Will's hair blew straight up from his head, like a punk's.

An airplane flew overhead. It might be coming from Hawaii. Hundreds of people were inside, maybe her parents, but from down here the plane was no bigger than a silver dot. T.J. craned her neck, watching it disappear. A streak of vapor trailed behind, straight as a chalk mark in the blue sky. Then that, too, began to fade away.

The ocean was a darker blue than the sky, choppy, with whitecaps and patches of brownish pink where snarls of kelp floated near the surface. Farther out, huge waves broke against the rocks, throwing veils of spray high into the air. *Spindrift* was what Uncle Will called that wind-blown froth. When T.J. slitted her eyes, it looked like white sails on a ghostly galleon. Unreal. She opened her eyes wide again and the mirage ship vanished.

Just because something disappears from sight doesn't mean it never existed. The airplane and the vapor trail were gone now, too, but they'd been real. And so was the stowaway. It didn't matter that she had not learned his name. She believed in him. He was T.J.'s Ghost.

What a mega title for a book! But T.J. knew she would never tell Jana. Some things were too special to share, even with your best friend.

Auntie Onion left Uncle Will to prowl the beach by himself and joined T.J. on the log. "Fog," she remarked, pointing beyond the breakers to the streak of gray that edged the horizon. "Out there waiting. 'The fog comes on little cat feet.' "

"What?"

"It's the start of a poem," said Auntie Onion.

" 'The fog comes on little cat feet,' " T.J. repeated. She had never heard her aunt quote poetry before. That was Uncle Will's trick. But this line of Auntie Onion's was perfect. Cats and fog belonged together. However old she got to be, she would never think of one without the other. "I wish the kittens had opened their eyes so I knew the colors," she said.

"Can't rush nature, or cats either," Auntie Onion answered. "Anyhow, they'd all be blue-eyed at first."

T.J. turned to her aunt. "Something else has been bothering me."

"That's what I figured. I didn't just fall off the turnip truck, you know."

T.J. grinned. If she could just stay here another week, she'd have as many words on her list as there were in the dictionary. "It's about the calico kitten. I'd like to name it Stowaway."

"Go away?" Auntie Onion's hearing aid jiggled up and down as she nodded her head. "Have to find homes for that whole litter pretty soon."

"STOWAWAY!" T.J. shouted so that Auntie Onion could hear her above the rumble of the waves. "Maybe Winston could keep her."

"Winston?"

"We had sort of an argument. I didn't even say ta ta."

Auntie Onion shook her head and polished her glasses, as if that would help her to understand.

"Ta ta. Australian for good-bye," said T.J. "You could tell Winston that Stowaway's from me. A special apology."

"Well . . ."

Auntie Onion bent forward and shaded her eyes. Uncle Will was coming back down the beach. It didn't look as if he had found anything, because he was holding up his watch in one hand and pointing to it with the other.

"Well," said Auntie Onion again, "if that suits Wilfred . . ." She stopped and smiled at T.J. ". . . why, then suit yourself!"

T.J. gave her a hug. Dear-Old-Auntie-Onion!

ABOUT THIS BOOK

Much of this book is true.

The lighthouse at Pigeon Point was constructed because of the many shipwrecks along this treacherous stretch of the Pacific. It is both the oldest and the tallest on the west coast, and has been restored to look as it did one hundred years ago.

The Giant Dipper roller coaster and the merry-go-round at the Santa Cruz Boardwalk are both designated national historic landmarks, and Año Nuevo State Park is the only place in the world where the huge elephant seals visit the mainland. As for rhyming slang, many of the original words and phrases used in this book are still used in Australia today.

The descriptions of the wrecking of the *Coya* in 1866 and of those who were aboard her are taken from actual accounts. Names and events are as they were first recorded.

There really was a thirteen-year-old stowaway on board the *Coya*, journeying to San Francisco to seek his fortune. Since his name never appeared in the ship's log, it could not appear in this book, either. If it had, then this would not be a true story.